The Ghosts of Kali Oka Road

Book One

Gulf Coast Paranormal Series

By M.L. Bullock

Dedication

For Nicole, who isn't afraid of the dark.

Prologue — Ranger Shaw

Mobile, Alabama
1983

Drinking beer on a Friday night was not Melissa's idea of a good time — as she let me know in no uncertain terms. Rather than prolong her temper tantrum, I appeased her by cutting our party attendance short and taking a drive. I tried to look on the bright side — maybe she wanted to ditch the after-game party because she wanted to show her favorite football player how much she appreciated the victory. And like any guy with a steady girlfriend would, I took that to mean, "Hey, let's go somewhere quiet and get naked."

She didn't fuss when I turned the car down Highway 45 and then onto Kali Oka Road. And there were no complaints at all as I eased across the creaking wooden bridge. She stared out the window and twisted her ponytail with her red-painted fingernails. I took that to mean she was thinking about us. About what would happen in just a few minutes.

And she didn't say a word when I parked the car in the lane and turned off the engine. Melissa had climbed into the backseat at my invitation, and now we were so close to getting it on, my heart was banging in my bruised chest. The only downside was that my buzz was quickly vanishing and she wanted to play innocent with me. Didn't she understand we were wasting sweet time?

If she didn't want to do anything, why flirt with me the entire drive up here? Watching her roll on multiple layers of shiny lip gloss, seeing her cross her legs occasionally to show off that sensational tan, and feeling her hand in mine just about drove me crazy. Melissa Hendricks knew she turned me on, and she knew exactly what she was doing. Who was she kidding? Now, just when things were getting hot and heavy, she wanted to put the brakes on the whole thing. Talk about being a tease. Maybe Beau was right, maybe I should call Natalie back and see what was up. Might be better than my weekly torture sessions with Melissa. We'd only done it three times, and we'd been going together for over a year now. I couldn't remember the exact timing, but she did. To the day.

"Get off me, Ranger! All you think about is S-E-X!"

"Why are you spelling it? It's sex, Liss. And we've had it before." Even in the shade of the dense woods around us, I could see her pretty face crumple in the moonlight. I sighed unhappily. "All I can do is think about you, Melissa. Think about our time together. You're the only girl for me. Stop giving me a hard time. I want to make love to you and hold those beautiful..." She smacked my shoulder so hard it stunned me. I sat up, feeling befuddled. Yeah, that's how I felt. Funny how I never thought

I'd use that word in a sentence. "What? Don't you want to?"

"No! I mean, sometimes I do, but not all the time. Why can't we just talk for a while? You know, like we used to." Melissa's ponytail was crooked; she'd lost her red ribbon somewhere in my backseat. Just looking at her made me want her, but my desire was decreasing steadily along with my beer buzz. Pretty soon I wouldn't have the courage I needed to make my move.

"Okay, baby. We can slow down. What should we talk about?" I rubbed her cheek lovingly and stared into her blue eyes like I really cared. As if I wanted to chat.

Happy that she was in control again, as if she hadn't been already, Melissa shrugged her petite shoulders and smiled awkwardly. "I don't know. Anything."

"Well…Let's talk about you and me. That's my favorite subject, Liss." I leaned in for another kiss, a second chance at crossing the finish line. She didn't resist me. I kissed her softly, reminding myself to go slow.

Keep control. Pace yourself. Geesh, I sounded like Coach Murray. I didn't want to think about that old man right now. Gross.

I mentally switched gears, thinking instead about my father's magazines and my sister's endless stack of Cosmos. The truth was I liked reading about sex better than gawking at pictures of naked girls. I had access to a naked girl, at least some of the time. I just needed to know for sure what to do with her. Seemed like whenever I remembered what I read in Cosmo, it paid off, but right now my blood was boiling with desire for Melissa. It was hard to re-member anything else.

God, this girl had the perfect body. Now if she'd just let me see it again.

My mind raced with images of the first time we made love. That had been exciting and not entirely expected. I couldn't help myself tonight. I wanted to relive the thrill, and I was amped big time from our win. The Mobile Mavericks won their first game of the year, and I had scored the winning touchdown. Didn't I deserve some appreciation from my favor-ite cheerleader? REO Speedwagon blared "Keep the Fire Burning" from the front seat, and it was quickly getting cold in the car. I should have left the heat on, but no way was I climbing back up there now. I might never get Melissa back here again.

After what seemed like an eternity of slow kisses and no hands below the waist, I thought I was in the clear. But as soon as I headed south, Melissa swat-ted my hand away and pushed my shoulder so hard I flopped back on the leather seat to catch my breath.

"Get off me, you pig. I knew you were full of it."

"Hey! I didn't force you to come. And it's not like we're the only ones doing it out here."

She sat up and gazed out the foggy back window, rubbing it with her sleeve. I guess she was trying to get a better view. A shadow passed over the car, but she didn't seem to take any notice. Instead, she frowned at me and said, "You're such a liar. There's nobody out here! Why did we even leave the party?"

"I didn't mean they were parking on this particular road. And for the record, I didn't want to leave the party, Melissa! You did! Are you losing your marbles or something?" I hollered back as she climbed out of the backseat of my Chevy Nova. I trailed behind her.

"Well, I must have lost them! I'm dating you, aren't I?" Melissa's face contorted into a cry. It didn't soften my heart—I had a sister who cried about everything. Tears were the wrong weapon to deploy on me. Now if she'd shown me her bra, that would have shut me up damn quick. I ran my hands through my hair, unsure how to resolve my current dilemma. At this point, I wasn't sure I was getting lucky. I felt so frustrated I just blurted my thoughts out.

"This is your fault, Melissa." An owl made a weird sort of screeching sound behind me. It must have been in the trees near us. It made me shiver.

"How is that? How could you being a sex maniac possibly be my fault?"

"Sex maniac? We hardly ever do it! Did you think that after doing it once I'd never want to do it again? Come on, Melissa! You're killing me here."

She flipped me off like she meant it. "Good! I hope you die, Ranger Shaw!" Her words sent a chill down my spine. It surprised me because she had never acted like this before. Something was serious-ly wrong—even if she didn't want to go all the way tonight, she didn't have to say crap like that.

"You don't mean that. Just get back in the car, Melissa. I'll take you home."

Now she looked unsure. "Why? So you can go pick up Natalie? Or get a phone call from her?"

I couldn't hide my surprise. How the heck did she know about Natalie and her late-night phone calls to my house? Someone had been talking. I suspect-ed it was Beau or his shabby girlfriend Hope. Hope had the hots for me last year, but I wouldn't touch her with a ten-foot pole. Not then. Not now. Some girls just didn't do it for me. She was one of them. That didn't stop her from talking about me. God, that chick was getting on my nerves!

"I don't want her. I'm not here with Natalie. It's you I want, Liss. I gave you my ring, didn't I? What else do you want?" Her tears were coming faster now. Melissa tore at the necklace that hung around her neck. She fumbled with the lobster claw latch but got it open eventually.

"What are you doing?" I said, aggravated now.

She slid off the ring and threw it at me. "Take your stupid ring back, Ranger! I don't want the damn thing!"

I was pissed that she'd toss my ring like it was nothing, especially out here where it could easily get lost, but I couldn't help but laugh at her. Maybe it was the beer or that Melissa wasn't good at swearing. To hear her use profanity was just plain weird and hilarious. I picked the ring up off the ground and shook my head. I stepped toward her and offered it to her, thinking my act of kindness would end our argument.

"Come on, Liss. For the last time, take the ring back and get in the car."

Again I heard the strange screeching sound in the woods near us. No, it was closer now. Was that really an owl? Or something else? I knew Melissa heard the sound too, but she didn't mention it. She was too focused on being pissed at me. And I hadn't even cheated.

"Why? So you can paw at me some more? I don't want to go anywhere with you, Ranger! You are a two-timing bastard!"

"No, I'm not! Melissa! You're being ridiculous!"

"Fine! I'm ridiculous! I hate you!"

I shoved the ring back on my hand, determined to never take it off again. Her response was to spin around in a huff and walk away. What was she going to do? Walk home? That was a laugh—it was five miles from here.

"Then stay out here in the woods. I hope you get lost."

She mumbled something between sobs but didn't come back. I watched her stumble down the path, her hands two tight fists. Boy, she was pissed at me.

"Melissa! Get in the car!" She still didn't look back but stomped away down the forested lane in the direction of the dimly lit road that led to the bridge.

Well, hell. Maybe I'd let her walk. She deserved to after what she'd put me through tonight. Geesh.

I stalked back to the car, my hands shoved in the pockets of my varsity jacket. It smelled like her hairspray and perfume. It was definitely getting cold out here. No way would Melissa walk too far. Her Members Only jacket wouldn't be enough to keep her warm, and she was a bit of a princess. Then I remembered she'd taken the jacket off in the car. Or I'd helped her out of it. I opened the heavy car door and cranked the vehicle to warm it up. Yeah, there was her jacket on the backseat. I rubbed my hands together and turned on the heat. I suddenly wished I had a cigarette. I wasn't much of a smoker, but I did it when I was stressed out. I sat in the car and waited for her to come back. Every few seconds I glanced in my rearview mirror, but she never turned around, not once. I watched her figure get further and further away.

Now what? I moved the dial on the radio and Sting began moaning, "Every step you take, I'll be watching you," and I felt like a heel. "Oh, can't you see…you belong to me."

What had I been thinking? I would never hook up with Natalie. I was crazy about Melissa. I loved her. Damn! I did love her! Even if she never slept with me again, I loved her. I banged my palms on the steering wheel. *Man! Beau's right – I'm so whipped.*

With a sigh of defeat, I put the car in reverse and eased backward until I reached Kali Oka Road. I turned down Sting's moody voice and rolled down the window to beg my girlfriend to get back in the car. But to my surprise, there was no sign of Melissa.

I stared in the side mirror and didn't see her there either. No way could she have walked so fast that she was already on the highway. And there wasn't anything to the east.

Except for that house. The one with the broken chimney and the crumbling walls. People said it had once been a plantation, but I found that hard to believe. I did believe the other rumors that terrible, unspeakable things had happened there.

A few kids at school, including my buddy Beau, liked to psych each other out—they constantly dared one another to spend the night there. There was even a saying, "When you're walking on Kali Oka Road, don't look behind you or the Shadow Man will grab you." As far as I knew, nobody had seen a Shadow Man or anything else on Kali Oka Road, on Crybaby Bridge or at the old Oak Grove Plantation.

But I knew for a fact that Melissa would not seek shelter in that old place. She was scared of anything remotely spooky, so much so that we had to walk out of the movie Alien. It wasn't all that scary, unless you were in space, which we weren't. I tried explaining that to her, but it hadn't mattered.

I parked the car and stepped out into the cold. "Melissa!" I called again and again into the chilly darkness, but I never heard a response. Not even a crunch of her tennis shoes. Nothing but that weird owl, the one I'd heard earlier, but it sounded even closer and larger than I first believed. Much larger. I decided that wasn't an owl at all but something I wanted to avoid. It flew over me, and its wings were so wide, the silhouette so dark it seemed like something dangerous. The word "demonic" came to mind.

And it was definitely stalking me.

"Melissa! Baby, come on!" I kept my hands up to protect my head and glanced around nervously. I heard a crunch in the tree line behind me, a few footsteps, and then it went quiet once again. As if it had never happened. Why would she hide from me?

With growing trepidation, I whispered, "Melissa?"

Something wasn't right here. Not at all. I heard a shifting in the dry leaves, like a wind blew through them, and then a thud, like a heavy branch fell to the ground. At least that's what I told myself. Why did I feel like I'd just stepped into a scene from The Evil Dead? But that didn't quite sound like a zombie's footsteps sliding along the ground.

"Dude, get it together," I scolded myself.

"All right, Melissa! You better come out now! No more jacking around. If you don't come here by the time I count to ten…" I heard a thud on the opposite side of my car. Was that demon owl dropping something on my car? Maybe a dead squirrel or a rat? It sounded heavy, whatever it was. As the menacing shadow flew away, I walked around the car; my breath was easily visible now, and it made a cloud around me. My nose was running from the cold, and all my earlier fantasies of having sex with my girlfriend had completely evaporated.

It had been replaced by a stronger urge, an urge to keep Melissa — and myself — alive.

A whisper encircled me. Did someone just say my name?

Ranger!

Yes, and that wasn't Melissa calling me. I was in danger. There was no doubt now.

And what I saw on the other side of the car proved it. That was no field rat or dead squirrel the owl had thrown at me. It was a hand. A white hand that was missing the rest of its body.

"Son of a bitch!" was all I could manage to say.

Then the shadow crossed overhead again, and this time I could see the black figure clearly. It had pitch black wings, and it tilted its head toward me as it buzzed over the car. The creature's eyes were set wide apart and red, but not the kind of red you see on cheap car lights or in the movies. It was the kind of red that reminded you of burning embers. They were burning crimson now, soulless and promising me nothing but pain as the bird opened its mouth and screeched again. Once I could tear my gaze away from the eyes, I focused on its massive talons. It delivered another thud, and a big, round rock landed on the hood of my Nova. Only this wasn't a rock. It was a head. A blond head with a crooked ponytail. I couldn't see the face, but I knew the hair. It bounced off my car and landed in the dirt.

Melissa!

I gagged with disgust and sobbed. Fright overtook me, and I ran for my car. As I reached for the door handle, the owl flew past and landed heavily on my shoulders. I could feel the creature's sharp talons digging into the thick leather of my varsity jacket. I was crying now. I didn't want to die or get hurt. I didn't want to leave Melissa behind, but I had no choice. If this thing would allow me to leave, I was gone.

"No!" I screamed as it tugged at me and nearly picked me up off the ground. And then I heard the second sound, the scream of a woman. She screamed, and the owl released me and flew toward the trees. I could see the screaming woman now; she was in the clearing, just beyond the old fence in the only vacant space in the trees. Her pale skin was as gray as death itself. She had black hair the color of a dirty, dark shroud, and it suddenly lifted away from her face as she shrieked at me. The woman's mouth was wider than it should be, and the inside of it was like a black cavern. She said some words, but I could not make out what they were. Her torn antebellum-style gown had no color and appeared dirty, as if she'd pulled herself out of her grave. A rusty broken chain dangled from her neck, and she bellowed another scream. It was a sound that promised I would die tonight.

I immediately began saying the Lord's Prayer as I managed to get into my car. I kept praying and crying until I pulled the keys out of the pocket of my jeans.

"Please, God! Please!" I pleaded aloud as I put the car in drive and took off as quickly as I could away from the owl and the screaming woman. By the time I stopped crying, I was turning off Kali Oka Road and onto the highway. I went straight to the police station and told them everything that happened. I didn't care that they would think I was crazy. I didn't care at all.

"Find my girlfriend—find Melissa!" I cried until my parents came to get me. They took me straight to the hospital, where I was put on a seventy-two-hour psych hold until the police department could get the evidence they needed against me. My parents didn't know what to think, and I felt extremely disappointed that they didn't believe me. Obviously they didn't, or I would have been home with them.

Three days later, I'd heard no news and had no guests. I would discover later that my parents were not allowed to visit me during the psychiatric hold period. It had been agony wondering if they'd abandoned me. I could only imagine that my Melissa was dead—murdered by the owl or the screaming woman. Or perhaps something else. She had to be dead if her hand and head had landed on my car. Yes, she was dead. Even with the psychotropic drugs they fed me intravenously, it was the only thing that made sense to me.

After I was released from the psych ward of Mobile Infirmary, two armed detectives came to visit me at home. They insisted I knew where Melissa was because I was the last person she'd been seen with.

Don't you remember that party on Presley's Landing, sonny?

How many beers did you say you drank?

Your friend Hope says she saw you in a screaming match with Melissa before you guys left.

Despite my "fantastic story," as they called it, and my insistence that it happened just as I described, there were no body parts found. No bloody hand or the head of my girlfriend. No signs of a freakish woman or a strange owl.

And worst of all, there was absolutely no Melissa. And I couldn't make myself go back to Kali Oka Road.

I never saw her again.

Except in my dreams.

Chapter One—Cassidy Wright

I woke up early with the compulsion to paint the picture I saw in my mind, images left over from my visions. There were faces, two faces — one of a dark-skinned man, and one of an unearthly pale woman with pitch-black hair. They needed me to see them, to paint them. They wanted to be remembered.

I had to be at work in four hours; it was three in the morning now, but I thought that would give me the time I needed to satisfy the compulsion. I immediately grabbed a water bottle and moved the easel over by one of the airy loft windows. I flipped on all the lights; it helped with the painting and sometimes tricked my brain into thinking it wasn't that tired. I padded off to the bathroom and brushed my teeth. That was another way of telling my body to fall in line. "We're awake now. Get moving." I wasn't much of a coffee drinker, but I could probably become one without much provocation this morning. Too bad I didn't have any in the house. Mike used to keep some around, but I'd booted him out six months ago. Him and his coffee.

"Cassidy Wright, you should go to bed and get some rest!" I advised myself in the mirror. Of course, I didn't listen. I washed my face quickly and patted it dry. The reflection that stared back at me testified that I needed sleep. Dark circles under the eyes didn't pair well with my pale skin and red hair, and the weird cowlick that I constantly warred with didn't help. I felt my mind drifting back to the image from my vision, the image that would remain there until I delivered it to the canvas. I put my hopeless hair in a clip and pulled on my smock. I slipped socks on my feet; the floor of my loft apartment was perpetually cool, even in summer. Now that it was October, well, that made it even colder. How was it October already? I felt heartsick thinking about it. October 23rd was a mere twenty-two days away now. Another year of not knowing anything about Kylie except that she was missing.

And strange how today was so much like the day she disappeared.

I had woken up early that morning to paint too. I had reasoned with myself, "Stay in bed. She can model for you later," but the urgency never diminished. And paint I did. I painted her face, and it peered back at me from a meadow of sunlight and flowers and butterflies, three of her favorite things. I was working on the last details of her eyes when I heard a knock at the door. A friendly police officer came to inform me about my sister's disappearance. As he spoke, I stared at her portrait. Kylie's eyes watched me as if she expected me to know something, to help her. I imagined I heard her voice in my ear and I fainted. That was the first time I'd ever fainted. When I recovered I immediately flew back to Mobile to await the news of Kylie's safe return.

Six months later I still waited. And then a year and then another.

We had no word at all. She merely vanished from school; the only witness to her disappearance was one of her classmates, and her closest friend, Angela Michaelson. After a few months Angela refused to speak about it again, and who could blame her? The media coverage had been relentless. They had stalked Angela, demanding interviews day and night. But all that changed after just a few months. Eventually nobody remembered my little sister. It was like she had never been born, except she *had* been born. I had the scar on my knee to prove it. I remembered the day I got it. It was a freak accident, really. I'd chased her through the yard as she screamed with delight. I fell on a piece of slate rock and sliced open my knee. For further proof of her existence, I kept her last lost tooth in my jewelry box. I'd been the one to put the quarter under her pillow. I knew our uncle would never remember to do that.

Our uncle managed to have Kylie declared dead two years after she'd vanished, which left him very wealthy. And me as well, but I didn't care about the money, as my banking account could attest to. I purchased my loft, but I did so only because I wanted Kylie to know I wasn't leaving until she came home and when she came back to me, she'd have somewhere to go.

It had been four years since I looked at my sister's portrait. The canvas rested at the back of the closet, facing the wall. I couldn't bear to see her sweet face staring back at me so helplessly. The following week, after waiting to hear her voice again, I covered the portrait with a sheet and eventually put it away. I had to if I wanted to keep my sanity. But I never forgot her.

And now it was 3:15 a.m. and I was experiencing the strange compulsion to paint all over again. I put on my headphones and cranked up my newest instrumental album download; this one featured a violinist I loved. In a few minutes, I began to paint. I started with the image of the woman. I stroked the long lines of her sinewy arms and then brushed on her dress. Yes, she was strong and perhaps once a handsome woman. With increasing determination and curiosity, I began discerning and then painting her face. She had an oval-shaped face with defined cheekbones and heavy dark brows that wouldn't be attractive in modern times, but they were natural and full. They suited her. Yes, she was a handsome woman. I stretched my back a moment and closed my eyes to drown myself in the lovely strains of the stringed instruments. I lined out her dress and dabbed in the various colors to create textures, white, off-white and cream, and then rounded her modest bosom. Whoever she was, she had been young, at least in this moment. As I worked and studied the mental image, I believed even more strongly that I was not looking into the face of anyone alive.

The woman had lived long before my time.

I glanced at the clock. It was now 5:20. Where had the time gone? I had less than two hours to finish this before work, and finish I must. I whimpered with desperation. I closed my eyes, and yes, I could see him now. Plainly.

He was dark, as dark as she was pale. He had powerful-looking arms and was much taller than she was. He would have certainly towered over most men too, but I could only see these two. And they weren't in an embrace or looking at one another. With fearful expressions, they were fleeing.

Fleeing from someone who remained just out of my view. *Hmm…keep painting. See what emerges.*

He stood behind her, close but not too close, just as I saw them in my mind, or wherever I had summoned these images from. Yes, he stood behind her, as if he would protect her as they ran through the woods. Woods I had yet to paint. This project was getting out of control. Four hours wasn't going to be enough.

I used the caramels, the browns, the taupe hues to create the shade for his burnished skin. No, that was wrong. I dabbed and blended a black paint and soon found the ideal color for the man. His mouth was determined, and he was reaching protectively for the woman who ran in front of him. I dabbed his eyes; they were moist and focused on something beyond the scope of what I saw. He wore a torn white shirt with blue trousers and black boots. They ran through woods that I furiously sketched. The man had a strong face, a smooth brow, wide cheeks and full lips. He was an unusual-looking man, and I still hadn't made up my mind if he was the hero or the villain in my portrait. It wasn't my job to judge—just record and paint.

I glanced at the clock. 6:35, and I had to get a shower and get ready. It wasn't like I really had to work, but it kept me grounded and I loved my students. I loved that they were excited about art and about me. Now I reached for the gray-green paint and began painting leaves on the bare brown trees. Under the couple's feet, I tapped loose pine needles and piles of leaves. For some reason, I decided to drop the paint and pick up a charcoal. I quickly sketched a house in the distance. It was a large house, not as grand as some I'd seen, but it was important to this scene. Somehow, I knew it was important.

I sketched four fireplace chimneys and the steps that led up to an ominous-looking front door. No, this was no mere house; it was a plantation. But something was missing. Something important. I studied the portrait and focused inward, scanning my mind for any clues I might find. I could see the woman, the man, the black windows of the house, but then there was something else…

My phone rang, and after my pulse stopped racing, I picked it up. I knew who it was, and from the tone of her voice, I knew I was in trouble. "Sorry, I'm on the way."

"Don't bother coming in, Cassidy. I called in a substitute when you didn't show up. It's eight a.m. You couldn't call me and let me know what's happening? It's not my responsibility to call you every time you forget to come in."

"I'm sorry, Desiree. Something happened and…" I stopped myself and rubbed my eyebrows. "I'm sorry. It won't happen again."

With a deep sigh, she said, "I'm going to have to let you go, Cassidy. You are a great teacher, but I can't have you not calling in over and over again. The students need to know they can depend on you, and so do I."

"Please, Desiree. I had something I had to do this morning, but it won't happen again."

She sighed again. "I'm sorry, but it's out of my hands. I've got to go; the school day is starting."

I hung up the phone, too tired to be mad at her. Too tired to cry.

I washed my brushes and arranged them in their stained jars so they could dry properly. I edged closer to the painting and stared at the results of my frenzied session. If this project had been for one of my clients, I would have been completely unsatisfied. The man's face needed more definition, more color in his lips. The woman's hands weren't quite right either. I breathed a sigh of relief, feeling the urgency lift.

I felt I'd captured the essence of what I'd seen. Unable to resist, I reached out and touched the corner of the painting. It was as I expected — it felt sticky. The paints hadn't had time to set yet. It felt like congealed blood.

And then I was in those woods, and I was running.

Running for my life.

Chapter Two—Aurelia Davis

1858

Buried beneath layers of linen, silk and brocade, my legs pumped furiously. It proved difficult navigating the unfriendly tapestry of the Kali Oka forest. Slender hickory and white oak branches tugged at me as if they never wanted me to leave. I cried out as a hanging vine slapped my cheek and cut my face. I tore at the wild vine of Bourbon roses; they ripped at my skin, but I ignored the pain in my hands. Even though it was well past dark, I could see light shining brightly at the edge of the forest.

And the moonlight will lead you home…

That's what the old woman had said to me. I would never forget the dark, shiny eyes of the gypsy fortune teller. I hadn't put much stock in her cryptic message then, but that was before I arrived at Oak Grove Plantation. Before I became the wife of Bernard Davis. Before I knew the depths of his depravity and his complete obsession with administering pain to those closest to him.

And the things he had done—I could never have imagined them.

Just a hundred feet now, so close to freedom. I could hear a carriage hurrying along the road. Dark bushes tugged at my skirts, as if they too would will me to stay here in this dark place. *No!* I thought as I pulled the skirt and ignored the sound of tearing fabric. I ran toward the sounds of the carriage wheels rolling down the lane.

It must be Jonathan! My brother has come to save me!

Finally, I could fall into his arms and be safe. He would whisk me away to a secret place where my husband would never find me! I had written so many letters, and I had Della's promise that she herself had carried them to the post with her own two hands. But I had heard nothing. After a few weeks, I reasoned that Bernard must have stolen Jonathan's messages on their way to me. He controlled everything, from my waking up to my lying down and everything in between. And now I had no doubt that after he discovered my second attempt to escape he would want to punish me.

"No!" I screamed, forgetting that I needed to remain quiet. I ran as fast as my legs would carry me, the smell of rotting leaves and wet soil rising up to greet me. It was a warm night, and there were animals stirring in the woods. Something small and furry ran across my path, and I gasped as I stumbled onward.

And the moonlight will save me!

The moonlight glowed brighter now, as if it heard my thoughts and knew that it offered me my salvation. Shafts of the unearthly glow filtered through the thick canopy of leaves above me. It made the shadows darker; the woods seemed to fully come to life now.

And then another shadow crossed over me, just above the lowest limbs. I froze and waited. My bosom heaved up and down as I struggled to breathe in my tight stays. I heard a low rumbling, a man's voice! It shook me awake, and I continued to flee.

The path opened a little wider now, and my skirts ballooned out as I ran pell-mell toward the road. I heard the screech behind me; the Devil's bird soared above me, and I let out a cry of fear. I continued to run, losing a high-heeled shoe in the mud, and to make my flight easier I kicked off the other. I cast a fearful eye over my shoulder and saw the bird of prey, the creature's black feathers spread out — the thing's evil mouth opened in a scream. It corrected its flight and dove for my hair, dragging its talons through the piles of dirty curls and sending me screaming to the ground. After it fought with me for a full minute, it flew away, but not far. It wasn't done with me yet. And a familiar voice, Bernard's voice, came from behind me. He saw me but pretended he didn't. This was part of his game. I didn't look back but crawled a few feet and scrambled to my feet again. My scalp bled; I could feel the warm blood streaming down the sides of my face. My clothing was torn in many places, and one of my breasts was exposed now, but onward I ran.

I could see the road! I kept it in my vision, and to my utter relief, I could hear the carriage approaching.

Unable to control my desperation any longer, I cried out, "Jonathan! I'm here!"

Twenty feet, fifteen, ten…and then the carriage sailed past, never stopping. Never slowing. He hadn't heard me—he didn't see me.

It couldn't have been Jonathan. He would never have left me! There was nothing to do now but continue to run—I ran toward the moonlight.

Five feet now! With what felt like my last breath, I bounded onto the road. I was unsure where I would go now, but at least I was out of the Kali Oka forest and away from the evil bird. "Jonathan! Don't leave me!"

And then a shadow towered over me. His dark hands were on my shoulders. He grabbed me and wouldn't let go. He shook his head slowly, his eyes sympathetic but unmoving. I pleaded with him to release me and screamed for help, but he was a wall, a statue. His eyes told me he would never let me go. He couldn't, or he would die too.

I thought I heard the carriage stop, but it didn't swing around to pick me up. After a few seconds, the driver popped the reins and the carriage clattered away.

And then he released me. I fell to the ground in a heap of despair.

Chapter Three—Cassidy

Cassidy…Cassidy…wake up!

"Kylie?" I tore the covers back and sat bolt upright in the bed. Of course, she wasn't there. It was just another dream. I fell back on the pillow and pushed the hair out of my face.

I had woken up to a power outage, which was hugely inconvenient as I seriously needed to wash clothing. I was a notorious procrastinator when it came to laundry. In the past, I had toyed with the idea of sending my laundry out, but I didn't like the idea of a stranger touching my personal things. I decided to take a quick load to the Hullabaloo Laundromat; it was on the next street over. I'd been there once, when I first moved into my loft and was waiting on my appliances to be delivered. It was in a tidy brick building with clean machines. Despite its strange name, I'd never seen a hullabaloo going on inside. In fact, there was only one other customer when I was there. Nobody bothered me, and I enjoyed the quiet rumbling of the dryers.

I wasn't going to drag all my laundry into the elevator and down the street. I just needed enough to get me through the day. I opened the kitchen window halfway and peeked outside. It was windy out, but then it was often windy on the third floor. It smelled like another day in downtown Mobile; I could smell the diesel of the city's buses and the street cleaners as they tidied up the city. Yesterday a mob of people had crowded Penelope Street. It was a marathon, one that I'd promised myself I'd participate in but never got around to training for. I used to love running.

Today, people were strolling the sidewalks of the newly renovated downtown shops. I was usually at work by this time, so I rarely got to see such sights. Then I spied Mrs. Peterson sitting on her balcony just below me. I poked my head back inside before she struck up a conversation with me.

Mrs. Peterson never missed an occasion to make small talk, and that small talk usually became gossip she had to share with the other building residents. Like the time she received a package for me by mistake. She signed for it so I suppose she thought she should open it. She'd been completely surprised by the miniature replica statue of Michelangelo's David. I tried to politely explain to her that I was an artist and wanted it for my small but growing sculpture replica collection. As if she didn't know by now that I was an artist—I'd dragged up a few dozen blank canvases during my stay here.

And my ex-boyfriend hadn't helped at all. I think he took joy in shocking her every chance he got. At first, I found his antics amusing. He'd break out in song at the park and serenade me. Other times he'd get on one knee and ask me to marry him. I never took him seriously and made him get up immediately. On the plus side, Mike brought me out of myself. He encouraged me to live life, not dwell in darkness — and after Kylie's disappearance that's all I wanted to do. I trusted no one. For a long time I thought every stranger was a criminal. Yeah, in that way, Mike was good for me.

But then he'd do stupid things like step out into the hall in his underwear to get the paper or insist on calling the neighbors by the wrong name, including Mrs. Peterson. Every time he saw her he shouted, "Good morning, Mrs. Pervertson." He embarrassed me to no end, and when I'd finally reached my tipping point with him, I was done. Now he was gone and I was left with a perpetually angry neighbor.

I stuffed a zippered tote bag with soiled clothing, including underwear, my favorite blue jeans and my coziest pajamas. *Yes, this should get me through the day.*

I could have just waited until the power came back on, but I needed a reason to get out of here. No sense in hanging out in the loft all day moping over my lost job. I walked to the elevator and remembered the power was out. *Duh, Cassidy.* Well, I needed the exercise too. This would make a good start for my marathon training. I peeked down the dark stairwell, my least favorite place in the building. Sure, there were lights in here, but it never seemed to be enough light and they were unreliable. And when I was in here, which wasn't often, I couldn't shake the feeling that I was in a tomb.

"Get it together," I mumbled to myself as I heard the heavy door click behind me. I patted my pocket. Yep. I had my key. I began my trek downstairs and thought about my students. It was almost lunchtime; I knew what the kids would be doing. This would be the fifth-grade class, my loudest, most boisterous group. They'd whine and work deals with me, trying to get me to let them line up for lunch a few minutes early. As if that meant they would get to eat early. Most of the time I gave in. We'd cut the class short by ten minutes, clean up our mess and head to the cafeteria.

My kids. My heart hurt knowing I wouldn't see them again.

A few minutes later I was out of the building and almost at the Laundromat.

I sighed and hoped whoever they hired to take my place had some patience. These were good kids. They just needed someone to help them draw out their creativity. Desiree was right. I was letting them down by missing class, and I'd let *her* down. I hated that because she'd been nothing but kind to me. My one last true friend. But how could I tell her the truth?

Hey, you know how I see things that aren't there and compulsively paint them? Yeah, that's happening again.

Only Mike knew my secret, and it freaked him out. But then again, he was a selfish bastard. Desiree knew part of my story; she knew about Kylie and her disappearance. We'd met at a restaurant. She'd overheard me telling Mike about my latest painting, and Desiree politely asked if I'd be interested in helping her develop an art program for the school. I'd said yes almost immediately and had been working at the Plesser Academy not long after that.

Maybe I would wait a few days and then go visit Desiree to apologize in person. If there was any way I could keep that relationship, I wanted to. Once Mike was out of the picture, all our mutual "friends" had sided with him during our breakup, and I had thrown myself into work.

Despite my growing disappointment with myself, I tried looking on the bright side. Maybe this change would be a good thing. Now that I had more free time, I could focus more on my art. I had some skill and could certainly make a living as an artist if I applied myself, to quote my Uncle Derek. Once I arrived at the Laundromat I shoved the coins into their slots and ignored the sight of my paint-stained hands.

And the moonlight will save me…

The words of the woman in my dream echoed in my ears. Who was she, the woman in the woods? Wasn't Kali Oka Road around here somewhere? Tapping on my phone screen I typed in the phrase, and a flurry of articles appeared. I scanned through them, emailed a few to myself and did another search. What was the man's name, the one she feared?

Bernard Davis. Aurelia Davis. Hmm…nothing. I tried alternative spellings, but nothing came up. I went to my inbox and began to read through the articles. I must have lost track of time because the washer beeped. I slung the clean, wet clothing into the dryer, popped in a few more quarters and continued my reading. Interesting stories, but nothing specific about the woman I saw. But then again, what would it say? Kali Oka Road sounded like an ominous old place. There was a section of the road called Dead Man's Curve where a lot of accidents happened. One of the articles also mentioned a "Crybaby Bridge."

I skipped over that section since neither a baby nor a bridge figured in my experience. What was the name of that place? *Oak Grove Plantation!* I snapped my finger and typed the phrase into the phone's browser, ignoring the puzzled expression of the young man behind the counter.

The first image in my search results nearly took my breath away. This was the house! I hadn't imagined this place, and that meant I hadn't imagined the woman! I rose to my feet and walked up and down the aisle, twisting a long strand of hair with my fingers. "Good God!" I mumbled to myself. I paused and kept flipping through pictures. In all my experiences, I must have painted at least half a dozen paintings and had never imagined that these were real people or real places. Could all these scenes be real? If so, why was I seeing them?

Oh my God, oh my God. What the heck is going on?

I closed my eyes and put the phone away. A sudden breeze blew through the open doors, sending all the loose papers in the shop fluttering up and then shivering down to the ground. It was autumn in Mobile, and that meant random blasts of wind and often daily storms. The counter guy and I scrambled to collect the flyers and papers, most of which had come loose from a large bulletin board.

"Thank you," he said as we gathered them all up. "Most of these are old anyway and should probably be tossed out, just not in the street." He grinned apologetically, flashing dimples and green eyes.

"No problem." I helped him re-pin flyers and current notices as he began sorting through the older ones.

"I think I'll toss these. Be right back."

Only a few papers remained on the board now. Another unusually chilly blast blew through, and I tried to hold the loose ones in place. My eyes fell on a purple piece of paper. It was a flyer advertising a local paranormal investigation group called Gulf Coast Paranormal. This was an invitation to local residents to come share their ghost experiences.

Probably selling their paranormal services--or something.

I pierced the sign with the crooked pin, securing it to the bulletin board, and read it again. The address wasn't far from my apartment, but I didn't remember seeing a sign for the place. I guessed that wasn't the kind of thing you could advertise, though.

The counter guy returned after closing the doors. "I'm Joshua," he said with a smile and shook my hand. I tried to be friendly, but I didn't "do people" well, as Mike used to say. Joshua pointed to the flyer. "Hey, those guys are legit. I know the founders. You thinking about going?" Thankfully, the dryer buzzed.

"Um, probably not. I think that's me," I excused myself. I opened the dryer door even though it was still whirring around and was surprised to find that my clothes were still damp. So it hadn't been my machine buzzing? Oh well, I might as well go home and toss these things over the shower curtain rod. I stuffed the items in my bag and walked toward the doors.

Joshua stood behind his counter and left me alone. I paused at the bulletin board and stared at the purple paper. I didn't know what made me do it, but I unpinned it, folded the paper and shoved it in my pocket. I ignored Joshua's smile, offered a head nod and left the Laundromat, hoping to beat the rain home.

By the time I arrived, my clean clothes and I were drenched. At least the power was back on. I took the elevator up and disappeared into my comfortable, safe apartment.

Chapter Four—Cassidy

Gulf Coast Paranormal didn't make their place easy to find, but eventually I followed a couple holding a similar flyer down a narrow flight of stairs and into a basement. Apparently, I was at the right place. There were about twenty-five people crammed in here, and four of them were wearing black shirts with GCP stamped in gold on the front and back. I looked around the room to see if I could spot a pile of t-shirts. Maybe that was what this was about? A t-shirt fundraiser for the local ghost hunting group? I didn't see any shirts or other products.

I took a seat in the back, still unsure as to why I was here. This had been a strange day. Why not finish it with a bang?

I pulled my plaid jacket around me tight. It was chilly in here. I hoped they turned the heat on or closed the door soon. No luck. People were still coming in. How many folks were coming to this thing?

"Is this seat taken?" a young woman with rich, dark curls asked.

"No."

She sat down beside me and immediately began chatting with the woman in front of her. Obviously, this wasn't their first time to attend one of these things. God, I hoped this wasn't some wacky spiritualist group. I eyeballed the door to make sure it wasn't locked.

Everything seemed okay. We'd just have to see, wouldn't we?

"All right, let's get this meeting started. Thanks for coming out tonight, everyone. We're so anxious to hear about your experiences and talk to you about our agenda for the coming year. If this is your first time, raise your hand. I'd like to introduce you to everyone. Do we have any first-timers here?" The dark-haired woman beside me stared at me, and I stared back. She cleared her throat and smiled.

Thanks for outing me, lady.

Luckily I wasn't the only newbie here. An older guy wearing an Army t-shirt on the other side of the room raised his hand.

"Glad you could make it. Let me introduce myself and the rest of our team. I'm Sara Springfield, the co-founder of GCP." A polite sprinkling of applause filled the basement.

"I'd like you to meet Joshua McBride. Stand up, Josh. He's our resident techie and something of a genius when it comes to ghost hunting technology." Oh, heck. That was the guy from the Laundromat! Joshua grinned at everyone and sat back down. He didn't appear to notice me, and I considered scampering out the door now. As Sara continued with Joshua's resume, I studied him a little closer. He had short blond hair that he wore in a "waxed" mess, as was the current style for Hollywood heart-throbs and the like. He had sculpted lips and a square jaw. No doubt Joshua had a handsome face, but I suspected that like most good-looking men, he knew it.

"Next on our team is Sierra McBride. Sierra has a unique gift; she's a sensitive and also an award-winning photographer. She's been with GCP for what, three years now? We feel so lucky to have her with us." There was another round of applause, and Sierra waved as she sat. Joshua nudged her playfully. McBride. Right, she had to be his wife.

"And this is Peter Broadus." I noticed that Sara didn't ask him to stand. Instead, she stood behind him and put her hand on his shoulder, patting it. "He's the newest member of our team; we stole him from Paranormal International." The crowd chuckled, and he smiled awkwardly at the mention. Peter didn't look like the kind of guy who smiled much. "He does an excellent job with video recording. As those of you who follow us on YouTube know, Peter is brilliant at capturing not only interesting images but also sounds and even voices." Everyone clapped again, and Sara returned to her spot at the television monitor that hung on the wall behind her.

"I am sure some of you came to see Midas, but I'm afraid he's not going to make it tonight." There was an audible groan from the audience, and I glanced at the lady beside me. She was clearly disappointed and ready to leave. And leave she did, along with the lady in front of her. I nudged out of the way and hoped she wouldn't run me over trying to get to the door. Their exit did not go unnoticed, but Sara didn't acknowledge them.

"Thanks again for being with us tonight. Now that you know who we are, let me tell you what we do. Gulf Coast Paranormal is an investigative team, but we're not strictly ghost hunters. We're interested in all aspects of the supernatural, including cryptids, doppelgangers, shadow people—you name it. And unlike some folks you might see on TV, we take each case seriously and never charge our clients." Sara perched on the edge of the big wooden desk. She appeared very comfortable talking to a room full of strangers.

"Five years ago today we began investigating the Gulf Coast, and we've faithfully shared our findings on the GCP website and on our social media platforms. Our goal is to approach each case in a unique way and help those involved find closure or get a better understanding of what's happening to them. We do that through our investigative techniques, and I'm happy to say we have made so many friends along the way. Since we've had such a great turnout tonight and we want to make sure we talk to each of you, please fill out this brief form. We'd like to get to know all of you. In fact, we have some dates available for a few more investigations this spring. In order to meet everyone, we'll have to limit these sessions to a few minutes each. Then the team and I will get together later and decide which encounters we'll investigate further. From that smaller list, we'll pick a few and then contact the ones we've selected. Even if we don't get to you this spring, we may schedule you for this summer."

Joshua began handing out forms while Sierra gave out pens with Gulf Coast Paranormal printed on the sides. She smiled as she passed me. I liked her immediately. "Thanks," I said as I stared at the form. Did I really want to do this? I wasn't here for an investigation, I'd just been curious or bored. Well, why not? I was here. Maybe I could find out something about Kali Oka Road. I scribbled my first name on the paper and jotted down my house phone. I never answered it anyway.

Sierra and Joshua collected all our forms and put them in a clear bowl on the desk. "I promise we'll call each one of you, and we will stay until we're through. Remember to keep it as short as possible. There are refreshments on the back table. One last thing: if we don't pick you tonight, please try us again later. We don't want anyone leaving here thinking that we don't believe you or that what you experienced wasn't unique or interesting. We may in the future contact you."

Each team member began picking names out of the bowl. Apparently, it was luck of the draw. I would have preferred to talk to Sierra, but that did not appear to be an option. The GCP team called a few names, and individuals from the waiting crowd came forward and stepped off to the side for private conversations. I heard the side door open and close beside me. I guessed a few others were leaving too. I didn't look back but kept watching the interviews. True to her word, Sara kept the sessions short. She called another round of names and thankfully none of them were mine. I found a brochure on the floor in front of me and began flipping through it. I waited another five minutes and twisted the strap of my purse nervously, wondering what the heck I would say if they called me.

Hi, my name is Cassidy, and I'm bat-crap crazy. I see images in my head and paint pictures of them. Have you ever heard of Kali Oka Road?

Nope. Not going to happen. I couldn't do it. The last person I had confided in left me high and dry after he humiliated me to the utmost. Well, technically I threw him out, but only after he told me he thought I was having a mental breakdown.

"Cassidy?" Sierra called from the front. The sinking feeling in the pit of my stomach told me to get up and leave. I obeyed and only paused in the doorway when she called my name a second time. I didn't look back.

I'd deal with my compulsion somehow. These people couldn't help me. They wanted to look for ghosts and Bigfoot, not listen to troubled artists. Well, I'd been curious and I checked it out. Let them move on to bigger and better things.

I'd be okay. I'd figure it out.

Somehow.

Chapter Five—Midas Demopolis

I'd been surveying tonight's gathering for the past fifteen minutes, and Sara had done a great job. As usual. Although the head count was high, about thirty people, I wasn't sure how successful we'd be. I recognized many of these faces. Most were just fans. No, this was going to be slim pickings.

Or maybe I was just more jaded. Thanks to a local television station, everyone in Mobile knew we were looking for places to investigate. The station featured us when we documented activity at a local lighthouse last month. It had been exciting at the time, but rather than bringing in more cases we'd gained a whole slew of looky-loos.

And not everyone here was on the level, but that was true for most of these community meetings. I recognized a few faces; some were repeat customers who showed up at every one of these events with a new "experience" to share with us. And then there were local business owners who wanted to tap into the paranormal crowd by having us classify their establishments as haunted. The label "haunted" carried a lot of weight these days. I didn't mind that, as long as the business reps didn't hand me a load of BS. Like the one from Welford House. That guy thought he could pay us to get what he wanted. He had been wrong. In the end, I told him off.

Peter Broadus didn't like it because that had been his connection, but I didn't give a damn. As long as we were still GCP, I would call the shots. Well, Sara and I.

I took a few sips of murky black coffee and almost immediately pitched the remainder of the cup in the garbage can. I leaned against the back wall and watched the team work. Sara glanced at me but kept her focus on the person in front of her. Man, this was awkward. Would it get any better? How could we keep GCP together if Sara and I couldn't find a way to be friends again? I hoped we could do that because this was my life. Maybe my father was right. It was time to grow up and move on.

"You aren't getting any younger, Midas. You'll be thirty soon. It's not too late to help out your old man."

I watched the redhead walk to the door when Sierra called the name Cassidy. The attractive young woman rose nervously and was obviously having second thoughts about talking to us. If she hadn't paused in the doorway, I probably wouldn't have followed her outside, but she did. She slid her leather purse strap up on her shoulder and folded her arms across her chest. Like the investigator I was, I studied her for a few seconds. She wore a red, white and black plaid jacket, worn but stylish blue jeans and hiking boots that had hardly any wear on them.

She reminded me of Sara — and not just because of her hair color. She reminded me of how Sara used to be before fame and fortune went to her head. Who would believe that landing one small role as an extra on a low-budget film would lead to Hollywood knocking on your door? But it happened, and now my ex-girlfriend was leaving us to take on her new role as a lead paranormal investigator on a reality television show. She hadn't told the team yet.

"Excuse me, miss?"

She turned around with a startled expression. "Yes?" She glanced at her feet as if she thought perhaps she'd dropped something.

"Is there something I can help you with? I'm Midas Demopolis, one of the founders of Gulf Coast Paranormal. Are you Cassidy?"

"Yes. How did you know?" She clutched the strap with both hands as if she thought I was planning to rob her. I didn't take it personally. She didn't trust me, and I couldn't blame her. You don't get far trusting strangers.

"I heard Sierra call that name a few times, and I assumed it was yours. Most of the folks left in there were men, and I doubt any of them were named Cassidy."

"That's very astute of you..."

"Midas," I reminded her. "Midas Demopolis."

"That's very astute of you, Midas. Yes, my name is Cassidy, but I don't think this is right for me. I think you guys are looking for supernatural encounters, and that's really not what is happening to me. At least, I don't think it is."

"I'd like to hear about your experience. Not all paranormal activity involves ghosts, you know. And maybe what you have encountered is more common than you think."

To that, she gave a hearty laugh. "Oh, I doubt it." Her voice took on a mocking tone, but I could sense that wasn't how she really felt. She was weighing me out, trying to determine if I was serious or not. The more she talked, the more I wanted to hear her story. This girl had a secret, and the residue of the supernatural clung to her like an invisible wrapping paper.

We stood awkwardly on the sidewalk for a minute and I said, "I am sure we all seem a bit silly to you. Believe me, I've heard it all before, 'What's a bunch of adults doing traipsing around old houses looking for ghosts or lurking around swamps looking for cryptids? They must believe in fairy tales.' My answer to that is not everything that happens to us can be explained away with science or found in the pages of a textbook, Cassidy. Sometimes things happen to us and there is no explanation. At least not a 'reasonable' one. That's where we come in. We're here to help."

She breathed a visible sigh of relief and then quickly added, "If I did talk to one of you, I wouldn't want to be on television or on any social media sites. I want my privacy. It is important to me. I've been through enough."

I believed every word she said. And she did have a story I wanted to hear. I studied her face. Cassidy had lush red hair, the rare sort of red that many women tried for at the beauty salon but rarely achieved. She had almond-shaped green eyes that were almost hazel and I bet were changeable with her moods. She had an oval-shaped face with even lips that probably turned up into a beautiful smile. But I got the feeling she didn't smile much.

"I can appreciate that. How do you feel about going for a cup of coffee? There's Demeter's on the corner. No strings. If you feel like talking, you can. If not, you can go home and I'll never bother you again."

She chewed her bottom lip and looked intently up into my face. I was easily a foot taller than she was; I hoped she didn't feel intimidated by my size.

"All right. Just coffee. No promises."

"Great. Let's go." We walked along the broken sidewalk to the coffee shop; it was only a block away. She shoved her hands in her pockets and tossed her hair behind her shoulders. "You aren't what I expected, Midas Demopolis. None of you are."

I laughed at that. "What do you mean? That we're not covered in gadgets or wearing pocket protectors?"

"No." For the first time, I saw the glimmer of a wistful smile. "It's not that. And for the record, 'nerdiness' doesn't bother me. It's just that I believe you guys really care about the people who come to see you. I wasn't expecting that."

"Well, thanks, and we do care. Encounters with the supernatural can be truly terrifying if you don't understand what's happening. I wouldn't do this if I didn't care." I couldn't explain to her how true that was. I'd taken a lot of heat from my rather extensive family over my "hobby," as they liked to call it. In the Demopolis family, I was little better than my cousin Gordon, the funeral director. But then again my family had a deep aversion for the mystical. They were very religious—Greek Orthodox—and they liked to remind me every holiday and family event that by dabbling with the paranormal I endangered my immortal soul.

I believed just the opposite. I believed that by helping others find answers I was redeeming it. And in ways they wouldn't understand.

Cassidy and I paused outside Demeter's, and I followed her lead. I didn't want to force her to talk or come inside. Sometimes you have to decide these things for yourself.

With a cautious voice, she said, "Okay, I'm ready to talk, Midas Demopolis. I don't know why, but I'm willing to trust you with my deepest, darkest secret. That isn't something I do every day. I want you to know that."

"I believe you, Cassidy."

"Great. But I'm warning you, this might be a first. I guarantee you haven't heard anything like this before."

"Challenge accepted," I said, trying to lighten up her sudden intensity. Man, it was getting cold out here.

"And one more thing," she said as we lingered by the door. I could see our breath now. Was it supposed to be this cold tonight? "Coffee is on me."

"Well, that truly will be a first," I replied with a smile. Together we stepped inside Demeter's, and I was glad to leave the chilly air behind us.

Chapter Six—Cassidy

The old man who ran the coffee shop was definitely a fan of Midas'. He greeted him with smiles and talked a mile a minute in what I assumed was Greek. He tapped Midas' cheeks and slapped his muscular arms as he scolded him playfully. Occasionally he waved at me, and Midas held up his end of the conversation.

The man suddenly turned his attention to me. "My manners. This is my grandson who doesn't call his grandpa in three days. I worry for him. You understand?" He had a halo of white curls and a wide, genuine smile. He was significantly shorter than Midas, but he also had a stout build and looked like he could take care of himself in a scrape if the occasion called for it. Midas took all the attention in stride, not seeming the least bit embarrassed by it all. At least his grandfather was a pleasant fellow. The whole interaction ended with him kissing the top of Midas' head. "I bring you coffees."

"My grandfather. He's my biggest fan. We call him Papa Angelos."

"I can tell how proud he is."

"Do you have family here? Are you from Mobile, Cassidy?"

"Yes, Mobile is home. As far as family goes, I have an uncle and my grandfather. My grandfather's in a home in West Mobile. He doesn't always remember my name." *Geesh, what a downer, Cassidy. Feel sorry for yourself much?*

"I'm sorry to hear that. It must be lonely at times."

"At times, but I don't mind so much." I couldn't help but compare Midas to Mike. This was the point in the conversation where Mike would search for a mirror or some window he could look at. That guy did enjoy looking at himself. Midas didn't appear preoccupied with himself or his looks, which was a surprise. How could someone so dang handsome not also be shallow and self-involved?

It was nice hanging out with a guy who didn't constantly bring the conversation back around to himself. Instead, my surprise coffee "date" focused his warm, brown eyes on me and answered every question I tossed his way without hesitation. I was beginning to feel like a newspaper reporter. I couldn't stop myself from asking him the what, who, where and why of it all.

"Have you been doing this long, Midas? Investigating the paranormal, I mean."

"It's been a while. Officially we began Gulf Coast Paranormal five years ago, but I was interested in the unseen long before that. I had my own experience when I was twelve." He laid his phone on the table, but not before turning it on mute and flipping the display upside down. I slipped my hand into my jacket pocket and put my phone on silent too. Not that anyone would call me, but he was being so polite that I wanted to return the favor. He sipped his black coffee, which was quite frankly the most delicious coffee I'd ever had, while I dosed mine heavily with sugar and creamer. No wonder Midas was so muscular. He struck me as the kind of guy who had a lot of personal discipline. "How do you fight the fear associated with the paranormal, or do you not have any?"

Midas smiled, showing impossibly white teeth. "Of course I do. I'm as human as anyone. Fear is a part of it. But with practice and a focus on the science, you can deal with it and keep it under control. Maybe that's why there are so many investigative teams nowadays with all this amazing technology. Having a competent team of investigators around you helps."

"I see." I was running out of questions to ask, or at least questions that I didn't feel weird about asking. He didn't pressure me and asked if I wanted another cup of coffee. "No, I have a hard time sleeping already. I can't seem to get my schedule straight." I pushed the empty cup away, leaned forward on my elbows and interlaced my fingers. "There are a couple of things you should know about me. My little sister disappeared four years ago, when she was twelve. That's when all this began."

"I'm listening." He slid his cup to the side and leaned back against the booth seat.

"I paint—and draw. Once in a while, about every three months or so, I have a dream…no. That's not it…it's more like a vision. I see images in my mind, and then I wake up with this compulsion to draw or paint them. It's like I have to get them down on paper and can't do anything else until I've recorded what I have seen. I've lost friends because of this, and now my job."

"Well, that is unique. I can see where that would interrupt your life. Tell me about the experience."

I tapped the table, wondering how to answer him. "What do you mean?"

"Well, are there any other phenomena that occurred before these sessions? Like a feeling? A smell? Anything?"

I frowned as I mentally scanned through experiences. "I don't think so; nothing obvious. Maybe I should think about that."

He smiled confidently. "We can come back to that. Tell me how you feel during the experience. Use just one word."

"Feel?" I wasn't prepared to talk about my feelings. Not like this. "I guess the word would be 'focused.'" He nodded and I continued, "It's like I'm feeling what they feel—and they want to be remembered.

They want me to see them. How do you explain that?"

"I can't."

"Neither can I. Last night it happened again. I painted a woman in pre-Civil-War clothing, a dark-skinned man and an old house."

Midas glanced at his grandfather behind the counter and raised his finger. The man responded by bringing us two glasses of water. I sipped the water and continued. I had to admit I felt much more comfortable now than I had when I first came in, despite the caffeine injection.

"I knew you'd been painting." He pointed at my stained fingers. I hid them in my jacket out of habit. "I didn't mean to embarrass you. I have a bad habit of noticing things other people don't pay attention to."

It was my turn to look amused. "I guess that's why you became an investigator."

He smiled again, and it was a thing of beauty. I tried not to stare at his flawless skin and the shimmering silver chain at his neck.

"Probably so."

After a few awkward moments of fidgeting in my seat, I asked, "Do you have any other questions for me yet?"

"Not yet. Please continue, Cassidy. I want you to tell me whatever you want me to know."

I cleared my throat nervously. My hands felt sweaty in my coat pockets. "Okay. Today I had to go to the Laundromat. I met Joshua, the guy on your team. Well, I didn't actually meet him, but he was there. I saw your flyer on the bulletin board. When I got ready to go, I took it with me. Well, while I was waiting for my laundry to finish, I remembered some of the things the woman in the painting was thinking. See, this time was a little different. I touched the painting when I was done, and it was like I was there. I was her—the woman in the painting. She was a prisoner; her husband, Bernard Davis was his name, he kept her a prisoner in their house. It was a big house they used to call Oak Grove Plantation, off Kali Oka Road. The man, the one with the dark skin, was sent to find her. And there was this owl. It was like the thing was trained or something because it swooped down on her. It tore at her hair…I know I'm babbling."

"Take your time." He did seem interested, and he'd leaned forward on the table. We were only inches apart.

"Oh, wait. I've got some pictures of the house on my phone. Or a picture of what's left." I tugged at my phone and opened the browser. "Here. This is the house. And I painted it before I ever saw it. Only it looks a bit different in the painting. It's not a ruin in the painting; it's a new house." I handed him the phone and watched him survey the photos. "Please tell me you believe me. This is so different from the other experiences I've had, but this is the first time I've touched a painting of an image I'd seen."

He slid my phone back to me and stared at me. Those dark eyes searched mine, like Midas was trying to find the answer to a question.

"What's your last name, Cassidy?"

"It's Wright. I'm Cassidy Wright."

"And your sister?"

"Kylie. Kylie Starr Wright. Why? Have you heard of her? Tell me you haven't seen her as a…" I couldn't even say the word.

"Oh no. Nothing like that. I'm just gathering information. Have you ever heard of Oak Grove before? Maybe visited there or read about it on the Internet?"

I licked my lips, which suddenly felt extremely dry. Maybe it was the weather. "I have never been there and never heard about it. Only read about it today, when I was looking up the things I remembered from the vision. I swear I'm not lying. You said you would believe me." I couldn't stop the desperation from rising.

"I do believe you, but you might not believe this." He flipped his phone over and opened his camera app. "This is why I was late to the meeting tonight. I was taking pictures for an upcoming investigation. It's the same house, off Kali Oka Road. Oak Grove Plantation."

"Seriously?" I said entirely too loudly. I flipped through his pictures, astonished at what I saw. This couldn't be happening. "What does this mean? That I would see it and you would go there? And we don't even know each other. I mean, we know each other now, but…you know what I mean."

He nodded seriously. "And Josh never mentioned it to you?"

"No. He just introduced himself and said GCP was legit."

Midas tapped the table with his fingers. "How would you feel about coming to our team meeting tomorrow? We're going to discuss the Kali Oka Road investigation. Maybe bring your painting or take a picture of it and bring that. Tell the team what you've seen, and we can compare notes. Sierra's been researching the place. You might be surprised at what you hear."

"I don't know. I should probably look for a job. I need to get a handle on my life."

He shoved his phone in his jacket pocket and squeezed my hand. It wasn't creepy; it was affirming, and I found that I didn't mind it at all. "This is how you do that, Cassidy. Learn how to use your gift, or it will control your life." He released my hand with a wistful look. "Come see what we do. At the very least you might get some clues about the people in your painting."

"Can I think about it and let you know something in the morning?" I probably wouldn't go, but I couldn't tell him no to his face. And that bothered me. Midas seemed so sincere in his desire to help me.

"Sure. Hand me your phone again." I did as he asked and watched him put his phone number in my contacts. "Let me know something by ten."

"All right."

"And think about it first, Cassidy. Don't just say no because it's easier." He got up from the booth and extended a hand to me.

"I think I'll stay for a minute if you don't mind. I'll call you in the morning."

"Good night, Cassidy."

"Night."

I watched him walk out of Demeter's. I didn't have any answers—I had more questions, actually—but somehow I felt better. Maybe because I wasn't alone anymore.

Chapter Seven—Cassidy

I didn't call Midas. I wrote a text instead. I typed in a nice, polite refusal along with a thank you for listening but couldn't make myself push the send button. I deleted it and waited around until a quarter to ten to send him a text that read: *I'm on the way. Same place?*

I got back a short reply: *Yes. Glad to hear.*

I did get some sleep last night but tossed and turned for at least an hour. My stiff back reminded me that I needed a new mattress. I couldn't cover the portrait yet because the paint was still sticky, but I did turn it to the wall after I took a few photos of it.

The images were more disturbing now, and I could see where I had missed some detail. It wasn't a work of art, not in the traditional sense. I promised myself I would add the details when I returned to the loft this afternoon. I stepped closer to the painting, so close that Aurelia's face was just a few inches from mine. Although we were separated by nearly two centuries, she and I were close in age. My hand shook as it hovered over the surface of the painting. I felt a breeze stir around me, yet there were no windows open. I'd closed the kitchen window last night because I kept hearing strange sounds coming from outside. I used to toss bird seed out on my balcony until Mrs. Peterson called the landlord to complain. But it seemed the birds were back and probably hoping to score some more seeds.

Sorry, guys. Not this time.

Still, my hand hovered over the painting. Some force wanted me to touch it — wanted me to go back and see her again.

And I wanted to return to Oak Grove. I wanted to walk the halls and explore the forests. This time I would find a way to help Aurelia. Yes! I could help her! I must help her!

"Cassidy! Are you in there?" It was a man's voice, accompanied by a loud knock on my front door. It shook me out of my reverie, and I snatched my hand away.

What just happened? Is that Mike?

I glanced at my watch. I was late already, and I sure didn't have time for a Mike encounter. I grabbed my purse and headed for the door. I opened it without a greeting, closed it behind me and locked it before he knew what I was doing.

"Hey, Cass. You got a minute? I thought we'd talk." I glanced up at Mike's baby face, surprised to see that he'd grown a shabby-looking beard and had dark shadows under his eyes.

"I hate it when you call me that. That's not my name, and I have somewhere to be." I pushed past him and headed to the elevators. I banged on the button about six times in quick succession.

"Hey! I came all the way over here to see you. The least you could do is be polite and invite me in." That made my blood boil. I decided not to answer him, and thankfully the elevator opened. I stepped inside and hit the close button. Mike banged on the elevator but I hit the button again and was gone.

Why in the world would he show up here this morning? How did he know I would be there? As far as he knew, I was supposed to be at work. Unless he'd spoken to Desiree.

Once the elevator opened I shot out the lobby doors and headed down the street toward the GCP office. I didn't look back. Before I knew it, I was standing in front of the unassuming brownstone. Was I really going to do this? There was an old sign hanging off the side of the building that said Rogers Furniture. I hadn't noticed that last night. The place looked deserted and had dirty windows. I could see a few pieces of broken furniture left abandoned inside. I jogged down the outside steps and knocked on the basement door. Sierra met me at the door with a friendly smile.

"Hey, we've been expecting you, Cassidy. You can hang your coat up there. You want something to drink?"

"Thanks, and no. I'm good." I hung up my jacket and wandered over to the big conference table. Everyone I'd seen last night was there. Midas sat at the head of the table, but he didn't go out of his way to speak to me. He was shuffling through what looked like maps and talking to Joshua about topography and boundary lines.

"Good morning. I'm Sara. You were here last night, weren't you?"

"Yes, for a little while. Nice to meet you, Sara. I'm Cassidy. I'm glad to be here." If I had to guess, I'd say Sara was a few years older than me. She was a pretty woman with perfect makeup and dark red curls.

"Glad you could join us. Are you familiar with Kali Oka Road?" I could tell she had no clue as to why I was here. I didn't think it wise to tell her anything.

"Not really."

"Oh, I see." Her smile vanished, and she quickly turned her attention away from me and to Midas who was flipping on the big monitor that hung on the back wall. The two smaller ones on either side of it remained dark. "Looks like we're getting started."

Midas nodded to another man at the table. "Pete, cue up those recon photos." A second later, the image of a dilapidated plantation house appeared. I took a seat at the far end of the table and gawked at the picture. This was only the center section of the house; the outside wings were gone, making the place appear much smaller than the plantation I had painted. Some well-meaning person had installed two gas lamps along the front walkway, but they didn't warm the place up any. On either side of the painted brick lamps were two massive oaks with broken tops and crooked branches. There was nothing welcoming in this picture at all. Overgrown evergreen shrubs lined the sidewalk that led to the front steps, obscuring the house. It was like the place didn't want to be seen. Only one chimney remained standing; it poked out of the roof like a lone memorial stone. The top-story windows were covered with boards, and some of the windows on the lower floor were clearly broken.

"Before we jump into this investigation, I want to welcome Cassidy Wright and thank her for coming to hang out with us this morning." He didn't say more, and I could tell everyone in the room wanted to know why I was here.

"I met with our new client yesterday." He flipped open the file and read from his notes. "Ranger Shaw is a resident of the area but is not the owner of the property. A few decades ago, Mr. Shaw had a unique paranormal experience on Kali Oka Road. During the event, a girl disappeared, and she's never been found."

Peter clicked a button, and another picture appeared. "This is Melissa Hendricks, Mr. Shaw's girlfriend — the girl who disappeared. She was sixteen. Her parents have moved out of the country, and I don't think they are interested in hearing from us."

I stared at the pretty face on the screen. How could someone disappear without a trace? It was a question I'd been asking myself for the past four years. Not for the first time I thought, "We live in an evil world." I felt heartsick over this missing girl, and I didn't even know the details yet. Like most teenage girls, she had a hopeful smile. Her eyes were bright and cheerful, and the day she disappeared she was probably thinking of happy things, like the next game or a happy future with her boyfriend. She wore the red and white cheer outfit of the Mobile Mavericks and a side ponytail. Another picture popped up: a newspaper story about the girl's disappearance. Ranger Shaw was listed as a person of interest.

"Have any other people gone missing in the area?" Joshua asked Midas as he scribbled in his notebook.

"Yes, but that incident is the most recent." Midas continued, "Ranger Shaw's health is poor, so he couldn't come in person. He allowed me to record the interview and granted me permission to share it with the team. It's pretty lengthy, and in the interest of time I won't play the whole thing right now, but I've already sent you audio files. Check your inboxes. Cassidy, I'll have to get your email address if you decide to help us."

Before I could answer, Sara spoke up. "Okay, I'll bite. We don't normally have guests at these meetings. I'm dying to know what special skill you bring to the table, Miss Wright." She smiled through her taupe lipstick and repositioned her tiny frame in the half-circle chair to get a better look at me.

"I have to admit I am curious too, y'all." Sierra smiled at me. "Not that I mind having you here, Cassidy."

Midas glanced at me. I don't know why, but I stood up. Was I going to leave?

"I'm here because Midas asked me to come. I...I paint things. Things I have seen in my dreams. And I've been dreaming about that place." It was awkward, but at least it was a start. Nobody spoke. "The most recent thing I painted was a house, this house, the one you saw at the beginning of your slideshow. Only when I saw it the place was brand new. It had two wings, one on either side of the center structure. They were long and rambling with lots of windows. The whole plantation was painted bright white, and there was a forest behind it."

Sierra spoke first. "How did you see it? Could you explain that?"

"I am not sure how to describe it to you. It starts as a dream but evolves into a vision; when I wake up I remember everything. In fact, I can still see it all, and many times I get more detail as I paint. You know how when you dream you don't always remember the details? That never happens when I see like this."

"Interesting," Peter said. "Have you had this skill all your life?"

"No. I have always loved to paint and draw, but these sessions are different. This didn't begin until my sister disappeared."

The room was so quiet you could hear a pin drop. I felt like maybe I'd said too much. Sara said quietly, "Melissa can't be your sister. She disappeared in the eighties. Tell us about your sister."

"I…her name is Kylie Starr Wright. She disappeared from school. She's much younger than me, but we were very close while she was growing up." I shot Midas a look like, "What else do I say?"

"Tell the team about your latest painting. Did you happen to bring a picture?"

I breathed a sigh of relief. I was glad someone could think clearly. "Oh yeah. It's here." I dug in my purse for the phone, cued up the picture and handed it to Peter since he was the closest team member.

A minute later we were looking at my painting on the big screen. I heard Sara gasp beside me. "It's beautifully painted, Cassidy, but it is a frightening picture. What do you think this means?" She got up and hovered near the screen, as did Sierra. While they examined the picture, Midas glanced at me as if to say, "You're doing great." At least that's what I hoped that look meant. I'd hate to think he was thinking, "Geesh, you're a nut. How didn't I see it?"

Sierra shook her head. "You aren't going to believe this, but this goes along with what I have uncovered. I have to admit researching that road and the properties near the disappearance was a bit of a chore. The public records concerning the old plantation were destroyed in a fire, and what's left is vague, to say the least. I know who this woman might be…" Sierra walked back to her chair and flipped through a leather-bound folder. "Aurelia Davis, wife of…"

"Bernard Davis," I finished for her.

"Right, Bernard Davis." Sierra examined me evenly. "He built the house for her in 1858. He actually built it on the ruins of an older property, a house that has been completely lost to the public record."

"And was I right about the house? The wings on either side?"

"Yes. Now, this is where it gets sticky. There are three different rumors about the Davis family. The most prominent rumor is that Aurelia had a lover. A black man whose name has been lost, a slave undoubtedly. The story goes that Aurelia had a baby with this man and the anguished Bernard threw the baby off Crybaby Bridge, the old wooden bridge near the house." I shivered at hearing about such a crime.

Peter wasn't impressed. "Doesn't every county have a Crybaby Bridge? I wouldn't put much stock in that story. At least not the part about the baby. What else you got?"

Sierra shifted her papers. "Oh yeah. The second rumor was that Bernard was the one having the affair, with a local woman who made a living as a haint."

"A haint? What the heck is that?" Joshua asked with a nervous laugh.

"As with so many things in our southern culture, the meaning is varied. To some, a haint is another word for haunt or spirit, particularly a spirit that is attached to a person. In this case, a haint refers to someone who practices magic, casts spells, puts curses on folks. Kind of like Marie Laveau without the voodoo."

"Old Bernard took up with a haint?" Sara said as she scribbled something in her notebook. "If that's not an invitation for trouble."

"Another popular bit of gossip says Aurelia went nuts and convinced the slave to kill Bernard, but he got caught plotting against Bernard and the haint killed him. Apparently, in this story, Bernard had the nerve to bring his illegitimate son to their home, and Aurelia threw the baby off the bridge."

"Enough with the infanticide. What else, Sierra?" Sara kept her pencil at the ready.

"This story says Aurelia was kept a prisoner at Oak Grove. That Bernard forced the slave to 'guard' his wife. Bernard eventually grew jealous of the slave; apparently, the man had a soft spot for Mrs. Davis and Bernard had him killed. The wife also disappeared, but nobody could prove Bernard killed her. Not long after that, Bernard was found dead under one of the trees. And there you have it. Three theories. But I don't know how this story is connected to our missing Melissa."

"And there was an owl—a black owl. I've never seen one like it. Aurelia thought he was a demon-bird."

Midas picked up the recorder. He scanned through the audio and stopped after a minute. "Listen to this, guys."

A weak voice poured out of the audio recorder. "Something watched us. It flew over us. It looked like an owl, but it was all black—it had shiny black feathers and red eyes—they glowed like fire. I've never seen a black owl before." The man paused and coughed uncontrollably. I heard Midas talking softly to Shaw. "That thing dropped her hand and then her head on my car. It must have torn her apart. I never even heard her scream. But I saw the other thing. Oh God, I can't believe after all this time it still scares the hell out of me. It looked like a woman but dead, very dead. She had holes where her eyes should have been, and her mouth was...it was horrible. And she screamed at me. She didn't vanish like some ghost. I could see her plainly for a full few minutes until I got out of there. Please find Melissa; she deserves better than to be forgotten. I have to know what happened to her before I go." Then there was more coughing, and Midas turned off the recorder.

Joshua tossed his pencil down, clearly disturbed by what he heard. "I've heard of Ranger Shaw. Most everyone thinks he's guilty — that he got away with murder. How do we know he's not just playing some kind of sick game with us? Second question, how can we be sure this is related to what Cassidy saw? Other than the fact that the Shaw incident is in close proximity to the house she painted."

"Cassidy didn't know about Shaw's account of the owl, and it wasn't in any of the police reports. It's such a strange detail that it leads me to believe it has to be related." Midas rubbed at his eyes. "If you are asking me if I think Ranger Shaw killed Melissa Hendricks, the answer is I wouldn't help him if I did. He's heartbroken and dying, Josh. If any client ever deserved our help, I think it's this guy. He believes there's something on that road, and he wants answers. I think it's worth checking out, at least to bring him some peace before his passing. He's waited long enough for it."

Joshua had his arm draped over his head. He rocked back and forth in his chair and surveyed the room. "It's possible. But if that's the case, we're not dealing with your run-of-the-mill, residual haunt. That would make this a Class-A demonic event. Can we handle that?"

Midas closed his notebook and with a serious expression added, "We're just looking for answers, not trying to exorcise anything. Listen, if we do this one, I'd like us all to be in agreement on it. We work as a team. Should we check it out?"

Peter nodded and said, "Well, it's hard to say no when you put it like that. I'm in. I'd like to get answers for Ranger—and Cassidy. I'm down for another investigation. Does that mean we have a new team member?"

Now I was the center of attention. Surely he was joking. Even though Sara was two seats over from me, I could feel her bristle at the suggestion. I avoided eye contact with her and sank down further into the chair. "I have had no training and might just end up in the way. I wouldn't want anyone to get hurt because of me." Nobody argued me down. Apparently they also thought I wasn't up to the challenge.

Peter, who'd moved on from his question, clicked the next picture and mused over it. "Does anyone see anything strange in this photo?"

It was the image of a neglected cemetery near the house. I scanned the picture, anxious to see what he was talking about. I saw nothing in the trees, nothing in the windows of the house. Then I saw it. The gravestone had a deep etching, the image of an owl hovering over it. There was no name on the stone, but the owl image was clear.

"Definite theme going on here. Sierra? Josh? Could you guys see if there's any local lore about this black owl? Maybe a legend associated with it or some kind of news story?"

"Sure, Midas. How far back should we go?" Sierra asked as she tapped on her laptop.

"1850s to 1870s should do it. I'm not really sure. I'll leave that up to you. Sara, how about doing an image search? See if you can find this gravestone tagged somewhere online. And if there are any others like it."

She scribbled on the paper and nodded. Feeling like I needed to contribute something, I said, "I could sketch an image for you."

"Great. Let's meet back here this afternoon at four. We'll head out to the property and walk the stretch of road where Ranger says they parked. I hope to get permission to check out the house too, but if not, we'll at least walk Kali Oka Road, maybe down to the bridge."

"I can have it ready by then," I said with a smile, feeling strangely excited.

"All right, everyone. See you then." Midas closed his laptop and folder. "Cassidy?"

"Yes?"

"Leave your contact information with Sara, please. And if you wouldn't mind, text me your email address. I'll send those audios file to you."

I twisted my purse strap and chewed on my bottom lip. "All right."

"And one quick question, you are twenty-one, right?" He gave me a sheepish smile.

"Uh, yeah. Way past twenty-one. I'm twenty-four."

Midas chuckled. "I wouldn't say that's way past twenty-one, but good. That's good. There are certain insurance rules we have to follow on these investigations."

"Okay." I shuffled around wondering how to end this.

"I'm picking up Sierra and Josh on the way. I wouldn't mind picking you up too if you're close. Every minute the team can share helps to keep everyone on the same page."

"I think I'll drive, if you don't mind. We're meeting here, right? I'll just follow you guys."

Midas shrugged good-naturedly. "That works."

"I'll check in with Sara. I'll see you back here at four."

"Don't forget to wear your hiking boots."

I gave him a thumbs-up and went to face Sara.

Chapter Eight—Midas

I had a stack of paperwork to file, and I put in another call to the current owner of the Oak Grove plantation. I left a polite message and hoped that someone responded soon. Getting into the house would be helpful, or so I thought. By the time I stepped back out of my office, it was nearly noon and Cassidy was gone. Sara was closing up her laptop and getting ready to leave too.

"You want to grab some lunch?" I suggested. I hoped this would give us the chance to talk. This was probably the first time I'd suggested "talking" with Sara; she always had to win, even when we weren't arguing. But if we were going to move on and remain friends, apologies needed to be made. There was plenty of blame to go around for why it all fell apart. I should never have been so dead set against her Hollywood aspirations. At first, I laughed it off. Personally, I couldn't imagine doing anything else than GCP, but as she pointed out to me on more than one occasion, she wasn't independently wealthy.

"I don't have the Demopolis wallet behind me, Midas. Unless you're asking me something specific. Is this your roundabout way of proposing?"

I'd stammered and stuttered my way out of that line of questioning, but it didn't last. And once the Triton Film Company came calling, there wasn't anything I could do. She hinted once that she'd stay if we did take the marital leap, but that was hardly a reason for proposing. We'd been dating for four years, almost as long as we'd been operating GCP. For the first two years, things were great; we had our mutual love for the paranormal to keep us close. But then things went haywire. Our team grew, and we had the headaches of running a business — one that didn't charge customers for our services — and a complicated relationship. It just didn't work. But I missed her. I missed what we had.

"I'm no wide-eyed ingénue, Midas. I don't think lunch is a good idea. Besides, I think you've already found my replacement." She shook her red curls, and I tried to pretend I didn't see her silk undershirt peeking out from the open buttons of her shirt. "Take my advice, quit mixing business with pleasure. You won't always come out on top. One day, someone is going to break your heart." She stomped toward the door, her high heels clicking on the stone floor.

"Sara, can't we at least try to part ways as friends? We have other things to think about besides ourselves. What about what we've built together — Gulf Coast Paranormal was our baby. Don't you think we at least owe it to our team to try and work things out?"

"I don't think this was ever our baby. This was all you, Midas. Just as you've shown today. You didn't even think to talk to me before you hired another person? Yeah, save me the bull."

"What bull? Cassidy has a talent we can use, but I haven't hired her."

"You mean a talent you can use." She was visibly angry and not in the mood to have that talk, apparently.

"No, that's not what I mean, and I've never dated anyone on this team but you. Let's be real, Sara. Our breakup was your idea. I think you must have amnesia." Why did she always bring out the worst in me? My efforts weren't bringing me the results I'd hoped. In fact, I was making it worse. I put my hands up in a gesture of surrender. "What do I need to do to make you happy?"

"What do you mean? You want us together again?"

I dropped my voice and spoke as evenly as I could. "No, that's not what I'm saying. You have made it perfectly clear to me that your future isn't here. But I would like to keep things civil. I don't want us to part ways with bad feelings. I care about you, Sara. I always will."

She said perkily, "How very giving of you, Midas. To be honest, I'm much happier pretending to be your friend than actually being your friend. I don't want anything from you, least of all your friendship. I'm out of here in two weeks. Surely we can fake it until then." With that, she pushed the heavy door open and walked out of the office.

And that was that.

Chapter Nine—Ranger

I didn't answer the phone when Midas called. He politely left me a message informing me that he was indeed taking my case and that the preliminary investigation would begin this afternoon. He reminded me that he couldn't promise me anything, as some mysteries are never solved, but he did assure me that he'd do his very best.

What else could I lose? I didn't have a dime to my name, and even if I could work with this dang lung cancer nobody would hire me. If it hadn't been for my online work, I wouldn't have anything. And now I only had a few months to live, according to the crummy state doctors. My old man was right. I should have died in the Gulf War. At least I would have gone down with some dignity, not like a wheezing coward.

And I was a coward. That's what people said, those who didn't believe I'd actually killed Melissa. "The boy's a damn coward," I'd heard even my old man say about me. I wished I could disagree with him. The only one who didn't call me that was Beau. He'd been my friend all these years and never once called me into question.

"Come on, Ranger," he'd said when I told him about wanting to work with Midas. "Let it go. She's gone. Probably ran off with some college kid. You know how she was. Why drag up old bones now?"

"She was never like that, Beau. And she wouldn't leave her Momma. She might leave me, but never her Momma."

I couldn't make him understand that I had to know what happened. I had to know that I had done everything I could to make it right. After all, I had left her there that night. I was a coward. Yes, the truth was I believed it too. I left my girlfriend on that road. I left her there to get killed by that screaming ghost and the black owl. I left her, and there was nothing I could do about it. She haunted me in my dreams, her big blue eyes questioning me.

Don't you love me, Ranger?

I'd wake up screaming her name and sweating through my clothes. That had killed my short marriage with Ann Beauregard. "I can take a lot of things, Ranger, but you pining over a dead girl isn't one of them." She left me and our kid in a hurry. I couldn't blame her for leaving me, but leaving little Steve? That was just shabby.

So I had reached for happiness but never quite captured it. I left it on Kali Oka Road one fall night in 1983. And as death approached I began to think of Melissa even more. In fact, it was easier than ever to summon her face. At times I could almost feel her beside me, her soft hand on my shoulder. I heard her whisper, "Go back. Find me, Ranger."

I'd blown most of my minuscule savings on detectives and even asked a cop friend — well, I guess you could call him a friend — to investigate her disappearance, but nobody turned up as much as a fingernail.

Maybe Midas and Gulf Coast Paranormal would find her. Maybe they wouldn't. It had been a good idea at the time. I heard they did pro bono work, and since I was completely broke there wasn't any other option for me.

I picked up the phone to call Steve. "Son, you feel like taking me for a ride?"

"Yeah, sure, Dad. Are you going back to the doctor today? I thought your next appointment wasn't until Monday."

Steve's little girls were screaming in the background. Oh, that's right; they were going on a road trip today. I'd forgotten all about it. Damn medications had me so loopy I barely knew what day it was.

"You know what? You're right. I must have been looking at the wrong date. Sorry, son. You have a good time on your trip. I'm sure the girls are going to love Disney."

"Listen, if you need me, just say so. The girls can wait to see Disney. You're my number one priority right now."

Steve had always been a good boy, and he was a great husband and father. Unlike other kids facing similar situations, he was humble and kind. He'd never met a stranger, and most everyone in the area held him in high regard.

"No, I'm good. Got everything I need. See you when you get home." I hung up quickly and went in search of my keys. Then I had another thought. I picked up the phone and dialed Beau. He didn't pick up, so I left him a voicemail.

"Beau, it's me, Ranger. I'm taking a ride out to Kali Oka Road, going to look around. I was hoping to catch you, but you must be out. All right, talk to you later." I hung up the phone and had a mild coughing spell, then quickly popped the pills they gave me. It would only stop the coughing for a little while, a few hours, tops. Then I would be as tired as all get out. That was plenty of time to do what I had to do. Beau didn't return my call, and I decided I wouldn't wait. Besides, this was something I needed to do.

It was now or never, as the King used to sing. I couldn't die knowing I was a coward. I was going back to Kali Oka Road. I wanted whatever took her to know that I wasn't a coward, that I would fight for her. And if she could see me, I wanted Melissa to know that I loved her so much I was willing to face hell itself to find her. If I was going to die soon and was lucky enough to see her again, I wanted her to welcome me with open arms, not run the other way in tears. She had to know that I tried. That I wasn't afraid.

I walked outside. The noonday Alabama sun shone like a thousand lightbulbs. The old glass kind, bright and clear. I eased into my dusty blue truck. Once I'd planned on leaving my Blue Beauty to Steve—I'd hoped he'd appreciate her as he got older, but it hadn't happened. I'd leave her to him anyway, and he could do what he wanted with her. He'd probably sell her. He was always scolding me about buying a new truck, even offered to buy me one for my birthday, but I'd refused. "Save that money for something else. I love my old truck." Today I slid on my sunglasses, coughed into my napkin and ignored the red stain it left behind.

I put the truck in reverse and made the twenty-minute drive to Kali Oka Road. I thought about Melissa's laughter. Her absolute love for life. Her off-key voice. Her soft hands. Tears threatened to blind me, and I brushed them away. I pulled off to the side of the road before I got to the bridge. I felt sick and not for the first time today. But I surmised this was a different kind of sick. I wasn't sure yet.

I reached under the seat for my baseball bat and climbed out of the truck. I caught a glimpse of myself in the side mirror. I looked like death warmed over. I had lost so much weight I was barely recognizable to my grandkids. I had on a worn old denim jacket, even more worn blue jeans and my cowboy boots. For the first time in a long time, I had a strong craving for a cigarette. I wasn't going to succumb to that craving; cigarettes were what had gotten me sick to begin with. That and a broken heart.

A shiny red car blew past me, honking its high-priced horn on the way. I didn't care. I'd just as soon die like that than waste away in a hospice bed. Much better than drowning in my own blood.

I closed the truck door and walked across the bridge to the narrow lane where Melissa and I had parked so long ago. It was not used anymore. Who in their right minds would want to come out here knowing that a girl got killed here? I was gasping for air before I even made it to Lovers' Lane. The once narrow road was covered by bright green bushes and prickly vines that appeared determined to smother the countryside. No fresh tire tracks and no evidence of partiers, like beer cans or prophylactic wrappers. This place used to be littered with them. But that was a very long time ago. For some reason, I began calling her name. "Melissa! Melissa Hendricks! It's me, Ranger! Where are you? I never gave up, Melissa. I want you to know that." I walked deeper into the woods; tears were streaming down my face now, and I called again, "Melissa!" For a split second, I actually felt brave. Brave like I could actually do this. I could walk this entire lane and find Melissa.

"Melissa, baby! I love you! I always loved you. You were the only one! Melissa, please come out. I want to see you one last time!" I cried now, "Melissa, I'm dying. I need to see your face before I go. Please! Come out!"

I continued down the path, stepping over broken logs and refuse. Someone had dumped an old air conditioner out here. Who would do that? Tears flowed down my face, and I struggled with the feeling of hopelessness.

"Please come out, Melissa. I may never get to see you again." I was so weary that I held the bat limply. *Who would I scare with this? I'd never be able to swing it. Not if my life depended on it.*

I heard a crunching of the leaves behind me. Footsteps walked toward me and stopped just a few feet away. "Melissa?" I whispered without turning around. What if it wasn't Melissa? What if I turned around and it *was* Melissa?

What if she has no face, no eyes? What if her mouth is black? What if she's the screaming woman now?

I closed my eyes and held my breath and then turned around. When I opened my eyes and exhaled, there was no one there. "Melissa? Melissa, baby?" I couldn't understand it. I knew I heard footsteps behind me. I wasn't imagining that. No way.

A sudden wave of nausea overtook me. Damn cancer meds. They were almost as bad as the freaking cancer. More than once I'd had negative side effects from the many experimental medications I'd endured. At least now I wasn't throwing up, but I felt strange. Like the time I did acid with Beau and Hope. Yeah, that was horrible. I clenched my fists and waited for the sensation to pass. It didn't completely vanish, but I felt like I could go on. I didn't hear the crunching sound again.

After a few moments, I decided I had been wrong. Maybe I should go back and let Midas handle this. My strength was leaving quickly, and I felt a weird buzzing in my ears. I turned around and opened my mouth to scream her name again when I froze.

Melissa stood in front of me. Or what was left of her. She wore her white and red t-shirt jersey, her cheerleading skirt and tennis shoes, but she was missing her hands and her head. Her hands were mere bloody stumps, and her head had been torn off its shoulders. Bits of flesh and tendons covered her shirt.

"NO! This can't be you, Melissa! This can't be you! I came back for you! Melissa!"

Then a loud screech filled the air. The black owl sailed toward me now. The thing that I believed was Melissa collapsed to the ground, just as she would have done the night she was killed.

The owl dropped lower and lower until it was at just the right height to grab me with its vicious talons. I ran back down the path away from Melissa's dead body. How was that possible? How? I wanted to cough so badly, and I could barely breathe. I fell on the ground as the owl sailed past me, and then I rolled under my old truck. I would wait it out. I could see Melissa's body still in the sand not far from the truck.

"Melissa, baby. I'm sorry I ever brought you up here." I clutched the bat. I was steeling myself to face the creature. When I climbed out I would be ready for it. I'd pop it with my bat and escape. At least that was the plan. As I got ready to climb out from under the truck I felt a hand on my shoulder. "Melissa?" I eased my head around to see what was now with me under the truck. It was the woman with the black eyes and the black mouth. I saw her and screamed — she screamed back.

"Good God!" I tried to roll out from under the truck, but she reached for me and grabbed my jacket. I wasn't going anywhere if she had anything to say about it.

"Let me go! Let me go!" I said, swinging my bat at her. The woman was made of nothing. I was sure she was a ghost because my bat swung right through her. I jerked myself free, climbed out and stood up with my bat in my hand.

SCREECH!

I turned, and a second later I felt talons piercing my face. I was being lifted off the ground. And it all happened so fast I had no time to think about fighting it. I knew I was about to die. I should have died that night with Melissa, but somehow I had managed to cheat death. Not anymore. Death would find me now.

Then Beau was there. Standing over me. "Ranger, I told you to leave it alone." The next thing I knew, my bat was swinging toward me. Everything went dark.

Chapter Ten—Cassidy

On my walk home, I had a crazy thought. Maybe I should touch Kylie's painting again. Perhaps wet paint was the catalyst to entering my visions. I'd work on the painting, wait for it to set a bit and then touch it. I opened the door of my apartment and let the loneliness sweep over me. Sometimes I wished I had a dog or a cat waiting at home to greet me, but I'd never gotten around to it. Maybe one day, if life became normal again, I'd make that happen.

I closed the door quickly and locked it too. What was up with Mike? We'd been broken up for a while. I hoped his earlier "pop-up" wasn't an indicator that he wanted to wheedle his way back into my life. Now wasn't the time for him to reappear. I would never take him back. As if to banish any thought of Mike, I turned on Pompeya's *90* and rocked out. After pouring a glass of apple juice and snacking on a leftover sub in the fridge, I decided to give my painting idea a shot.

I slid the canvas out of the closet and placed it on the free easel. I lovingly removed the sheet and stared at Kylie's sweet face for a few minutes. For the 9,000th time, I asked, "Where are you, Kylie?"

Hmm…maybe I could add some detail here and here. Another dandelion near her foot. Another white cloud above. I couldn't bring myself to touch her face. That seemed kind of sacrilegious. With a careful mix of paints, I lovingly added the new details and stood back to see my work. With hopeful expectation I put my finger on the wet paint, but nothing happened. I sighed, and my heart felt deflated. "Well, little sister. I sure miss you. Please come home soon." I wiped a tear away with my thumb. I washed the brushes and turned my attention to the newer painting.

So this was Aurelia Davis. Such a lonely expression. I understood loneliness. The paint was dry now, but I still felt the pull to touch the painting. I felt nothing at first. Saw nothing. Only felt the dry paint under my fingers. I picked up a brush and dabbed on more color in a corner of the canvas. I didn't really need to add anything more. It was as it should be. Anything else I added would only be guesswork. I felt like these people deserved more than guesswork. Their story must be told, accurately. Except maybe the owl...

I put the brush away for the time being and moved the canvas closer to the window. Why was that window open? Could Mike possibly climb up here? I walked to the open window and stared over the brick ledge. There were black feathers on the balcony floor too, and more than a few. Something big with black feathers had visited me. What the heck? I picked up a feather and twirled it in my fingers. This was no ordinary feather. This was the feather of a black owl. It had to be!

My reasonable mind said differently.

It's a crow feather! Or a raven!

Sure, and I'm a six-foot blonde.

Was that creature following *me* now? I shook at the sight. Whatever was trying to scare me was doing a great job. As if on cue, my playlist began to play Atlanta Rhythm Section's *Spooky*. Heck yeah, this was spooky. My first instinct was to pick up the phone and text Midas, but that would be too much too soon. Still, I needed to reach out to someone. Even if I kept all this to myself. I glanced out the window again. There were storm clouds on the horizon. I came up with a lame excuse.

Hey, this is Cassidy. I'll take that lift you offered earlier.

Great. I'll be there at 3:45.

I sent back a happy face and went back to my current problem.

But…now I had some inspiration. I returned to the photo of Aurelia and the unknown man. I began to prepare paint on my palette. I found the perfect place to put the bird. That was what they were terrified of! It was the owl! I painted it behind them, higher and at a distance. I twirled the bird feather for inspiration and painted again. When I was done painting, I sat back and stared at the ominous black patch that lingered above Aurelia and the man. I wished I knew his name. Then in a flurry, I added a deeper red to the owl's eyes. It was a rudimentary example at best, but at least I had it done now.

I put the brushes in a waiting jar of water and stood in front of the painting. Should I touch it? I didn't have the compulsion that I did before. Maybe I could make contact only when the painting let me. The wet paint thing hadn't worked with Kylie's painting.

But something was going on. A soft whistle filled my ears; it was like a breeze blew around me, but I saw no evidence of one. Hadn't Midas asked me if I heard or saw anything before the experiences? I'd have to remember to tell him about this. How had I missed it before? My fingers shook as I reached for the black paint. Why? Why was I doing this? Without another thought, I felt the paint under my fingers. I closed my eyes, and I was gone...

"Aurelia, wake up. Wake up before he comes back." The pain at the back of my head greeted me first. Then my hands moved and I could feel a wooden floor beneath me. I could move my body a little, but I was definitely inside a confined space, like a coffin. Where was I? Please let me be home at Applegate. I'd rather be dead at Applegate than alive at Oak Grove.

The smell of cedar overwhelmed me, and I realized where Bernard had stashed me. I was not dead, nor was I at Applegate. I was in the chifforobe. Despite the beating, I had endured, I lived still. Blinking against the darkness, I heard Cope's voice, deep and low.

"Aurelia, are you awake?"

"Is that you, Cope?"

"Yes, it's me. I poked you some bread through the hole, but he's got this door chained. Hurry up and eat the bread. And don't leave a crumb behind or he'll know it. He'll be back soon."

"I don't think I can eat," I said as I rolled on my side and toyed with the bread. My jaw ached, and the taste of old blood filled my mouth.

Cope didn't speak right away, and I began to feel desperate. "Are you still there?"

"Yes, I'm here."

I scooted closer to the door and put my fingers through the hole. And to think I thought the world had ended when this corner got damaged on the move to my new home. How small and meaningless were my thoughts in those days? Worries over acquiring the latest painted parasol, where I would sit at the County Ball table, what poetry my husband would read to me before we blew out the light for bed each night. I'd been a fool.

Cope's fingers covered mine, and I sobbed. "Kill me, Cope. Break the chain and put a bullet in me. Find a knife and stab me through the heart. Please kill me. I can't live another day."

"Yes, you can. You have to."

Cope couldn't know it, but his words held so much meaning. Resting inside my belly was a baby. I felt him move sometimes, but not so much lately. After Bernard's most recent beating, I could hardly believe the child lived. As if he overheard his mother's thoughts, he moved and I sobbed again. I took the bread and shoved it in my mouth. It was only a few morsels, but I choked them down. Not for myself but for him. And why would I do this? I was only delaying the inevitable.

"Now listen to me."

"I'm listening." Tears slid down my bruised, puffy face.

"You stay alive. I'm going to get you out of here. Somehow, I'll get you out of here."

"No, you can't. He'll kill us both, Cope."

I felt his head knock against the door as he leaned closer. His voice dropped to a whisper. "Hattie is lurking around today, so I can't come see you again for the next little while. But no matter what…" Cope's voice broke. I poked my fingers out again. He squeezed them and said, "No matter what I have to do, what he makes me do, you know…"

"Hush, Cope. I know. Go on, before Hattie finds you here."

With one final squeeze of my fingers, he left. How much longer could I keep my secret? How much longer would I be able to protect this poor child? I fell asleep again and woke with the urge to urinate. I didn't dare do such a thing without my husband's permission. If I could not control myself, Bernard would beat me again. Only he could tell me when I could urinate, what I would eat, or anything else. But how long could I hold it?

I heard the sounds of footsteps approaching the chifforobe. Heavy and crooked. This wasn't Bernard but Hattie. She rattled the keys on the ring and opened the lock. The chain fell to the floor with a thud. The chifforobe door creaked open, and my hands flew to my face to protect myself from whatever cruelty would now be administered…

Oh God, have mercy on me!

"Cassidy! Wake up!"

"Mike? What are you doing here?" I shoved him away from me and scrambled to my feet. I'd apparently collapsed on the floor.

"I knew you were in here, and when you didn't answer I used my key." He flashed his wicked smile. "And good thing, too. I guess you had another one of your episodes?"

"You aren't supposed to have a key, Mike. I want you out." I felt half-drunk but not harmed from any fall.

He put his hands out as if to calm me down. "Hey, I'm doing you a favor. I figured when you didn't answer your door or your phone, you needed help. I'm telling you—those seizures are going to kill you, Cass."

"I don't have seizures—now get out!" I scanned the room for something I could use to protect myself. Never again would I be in a position where Mike could hurt me. Once had been enough.

"Your Uncle Derek sent me to talk to you. He wants you to call him. He's worried about you, Cassidy." Mike's smooth voice alarmed me. He never talked like that, unless he wanted to hurt me. He reached for me, and I stepped back. I noticed that the front door was wide open. Perhaps if I ran for it, I could make it. Although Mike wasn't making any overtly threatening moves, that didn't mean a thing. He was nothing if not dangerously changeable.

"What are you, my uncle's messenger boy now? I know what this is about. What it's always about with you. Money, my money. I want you to go, Mike. This is the last time I'm telling you. And leave my key."

Mike sat on the couch and patted the spot beside him, as if that would make it inviting. Looking at his eyes now, I noticed that he was high. High as a kite. "Let's not make a mountain out of a molehill, Cass."

"Get out, Mike. Get out or I'm going to scream my head off."

"Go ahead. Scream away. Let me know if you want something to scream about." Mike wasn't so high that he couldn't move like a cheetah. He was on his feet and in my face in a few seconds.

"You're high, aren't you?"

He stroked my cheek with the back of his hand. Repelled by his touch, I moved back and bumped against the wall. His hand went over my head, and he leaned closer like he was going to kiss me.

As promised, I screamed my head off.

Chapter Eleven—Midas

As soon as I stepped off the elevator, I knew there was trouble. Cassidy was screaming at the top of her lungs; I bolted through the open door to find some guy had her pinned against the wall. Good thing I hadn't given up after my three text messages.

"Hey! What the hell are you doing?" I yelled at him. Before I could cover the distance between us, Cassidy delivered a knee to his groin and down he went. Then she was on the ground next to him digging in his pocket. Grabbing his key ring, she tugged at a key and tossed his keys back at him. The guy moaned on the floor.

"Cassidy? What's going on?"

"He's my former…roommate. He's just on his way out, right, Mike?"

"Cassie, you bitch!" the guy swore at her as he tried to get up off the ground.

She didn't offer him any help. I didn't either. I was still unsure what was happening, but my hackles were up big time. Cassidy growled at him, "My name isn't Cassie. If you don't crawl your ass out that door right now, I'm going to use something much deadlier than my knee."

"I'm going, but that was a big mistake."

"*You* were a big mistake, Mike!" She followed him to the door as he limped out and slammed it behind him.

With shaking, paint-stained hands, she locked the door and didn't turn around. I could hear the elevator ding in the hallway and saw her breathe a sigh of relief. That guy wasn't coming back. Not today, anyway. And if he did, I felt sorry for him. Cassidy Wright wasn't what she appeared to be.

"If you need to stay here, I understand. We'll all understand."

She shook her head and flashed me her hands. "Let me wash off this paint and grab my purse. Sorry to make you wait. And sorry you had to see that. I swear my life is usually much more boring than this."

"It's not a problem. Do we need to call the police? Not to be nosy, but have you filed for an order of protection against that guy? Mike is his name?"

"Mike Barnett. It's on my to-do list. Thanks for making the trip up here. It was perfect timing, I think." She left the room in an embarrassed hurry. I could hear her wash her hands and shuffle around the kitchen. My blood was pumping from the sudden burst of adrenaline. I texted Josh and told him to give me a minute.

"Be just a sec," she called.

I tried to lighten things up by calling back to her, "Hey, I think you had the guy handled." She laughed from the kitchen, and I took the liberty of taking a look at the painting firsthand. It was different now, I could see where she'd added the owl. It blended perfectly into the trees, but it was more menacing than I had imagined. What could that be? It was obviously not your average owl. Some kind of First Nation totem spirit or an elemental entity? This case was very unusual—and so was Cassidy Wright. "I'm going to take a picture of the painting if that's okay. I see you added the creature."

"Yeah. Go ahead."

I snapped a few photos. It was a disturbing portrait. The couple's expressions were detailed and conveyed their fear at a level that I missed in the photos. I studied the lines of the house too. Cassidy had done a remarkable job of capturing the architecture with minimal strokes. I didn't know much about art, but I knew enough to know she had real skill.

She hurried in and out of the room. "I'm changing my shoes. Be right back."

"Great." As she scrambled down the hall, I noticed the only other painting in the room. It was quite different from the painting of the Kali Oka Road couple. A young girl sat in a field of flowers, with sunlight shining through her strawberry blond hair. She had a patch of light brown freckles that spread across her nose, a delicate cleft chin and wide gray eyes. This had to be Cassidy's sister, Kylie. If I hadn't heard the story, I would have thought Cassidy had been there in the meadow that day or that she'd created the portrait from a photo. It was absolutely lifelike—so much so that I half expected the girl to move.

Cassidy walked back into the room and caught me staring at the picture. Flipping up the collar of her jacket and avoiding looking at the painting altogether she said, "Shall we go?"

"Hey! Did that guy hit you? Where did that bruise come from?" Her hand flew up to her forehead.

"Oh, that? No that wasn't from Mike. That happened before Mike got here. I must have bumped my head."

"Really?" I asked, unsure whether to believe her or not.

"Seriously. I had a…I fell down."

Why did I want to protect this girl? Did she really need protecting? I wasn't lying when I said I thought she could handle herself. "If you say so."

We headed downstairs for the elevator and didn't talk any more about Mike. All she said was, "I swear I am really the most drama-free, boring person you'd ever want to meet. You've just caught me on a bad week. Is there a full moon or something?"

With a smile, I nodded. "There is a full moon tonight, and don't worry. My day hasn't exactly been drama-free. You aren't catching me at my best either."

"Oh, I don't know. You seem to have it all together." The elevator opened, and I held it open for her.

"Then I'm a better actor than I thought."

My black Cadillac Escalade idled at the curb with Josh in the front passenger seat. I opened the door for Cassidy and resisted the urge to help her up. I had to remember she wasn't just a pretty face. She might be only about five feet tall, but she was a stick of dynamite. I closed the door, and soon we were on the highway and headed to Kali Oka Road.

"Okay, Sierra. Tell us what you uncovered. Anything about that owl?"

"Yes, actually, but the information was limited. These large black owls are very rare, and some of the First Nation people refer to them as Night Eagles. As eagles are connected to the sun in their mythology, to the local tribes the owl was connected to the moon and stars. Interesting note here, the Celts believed that to see a black owl meant you were going to die; Romans believed that placing a black feather from one of these owls under your pillow would reveal your dreams to your enemy. But in the Creole and Caribbean cultures of Aurelia Davis' time, the owl was most associated with witchcraft and black magic."

"Witches, great," Josh muttered beside me. He seemed particularly on edge tonight, but then again he always did when we investigated anything besides ghosts, which he absolutely refused to believe in. That was one reason why I kept him on the team. We needed a good skeptic, and Josh certainly filled the bill.

"Look on the bright side. At least this isn't a nighttime investigation," I reminded him as I steered through traffic.

He grinned back. "Well, not yet. That's tomorrow night, right?"

"Yes, if the weather holds out."

"You guys want to go into the Kali Oka forest at night? Are you asking for trouble or what?" Cassidy shook her head in disbelief.

"Well, there's strength in numbers," Sierra said, always ready to put a positive spin on things. And that positive attitude defined her. All in all, we had a great team of folks at Gulf Coast Paranormal. I hoped Sara realized how talented and special these people were.

"So what's the history of the road? Anything we should know about?" I asked, curious to hear more.

"Well, it was placed on the National Register of Historic Places in 1988. The area covers 12.2 acres, which really isn't very much. It's technically the Davis-Oak Grove District. Points of interest in the area and potential paranormal hot spots are the Crybaby Bridge, Deadman's Curve and of course, the Oak Grove Plantation."

"Good Lord. Who names these places? Deadman's Curve? Crybaby Bridge?" Josh shook his head.

"I'm sure those are just nicknames," I said hopefully. "Let's stick to the area where Melissa disappeared and avoid spreading ourselves too thin."

Josh opened the map and pointed at a highlighted area. "So this area, right here. I think we should start on the road and work our way into the forested lot. Since there are six of us, let's go two by two, following each other, fifteen minutes apart. Sierra and I will lead and try to capture some audio. Give us fifteen minutes' lead time and then follow us in. Did you bring the bug spray, sweetie?"

Sierra tapped on her phone, "Yep, and I'm letting Sara and Pete know what we're doing. I guess they rode together." An awkward pause followed, and I tried not to grip the steering wheel too tightly. That guy. I'd had a strong suspicion about those two for a long time. Up until now it had been only a suspicion. More than once lately I'd caught them with their heads together, laughing and smiling. It didn't take a rocket scientist to figure out what was going on with them. Sara had already moved on. We turned off I-65 and onto 158. When nobody spoke, I glanced at Josh. He was giving me the hard stare.

"What? We're about ten minutes away. Give us the rest of the plan."

"Once we're all together, we'll reassess and go from there. Keep in mind that there might be old wells and other dangers we aren't aware of, guys. And Cassidy, it's like taking a walk in the woods, only we're looking for monsters. We won't be armed with weapons, just with electronics."

"That's comforting," she said. "I know it sounds unbelievable, but I know for a fact that Aurelia and Cope saw something. I saw it too. That black owl could certainly be classified as a monster. Hope you have some monster repellent too."

Sierra snickered beside Cassidy and elbowed her. If Josh was trying to get Cassidy's goat, he failed. He sure didn't know that just a few minutes ago she'd delivered a serious knee to the groin to a guy who tried to accost her. Josh didn't know who he was messing with. He cast an evil eye at Sierra over his shoulder but didn't say anything else.

I pulled the vehicle off the highway and onto Kali Oka Road. It was a two-lane highway with thick woods off each side, but the county kept the forest clipped back a good twenty feet. That at least was something.

"Okay, the road we're looking for should be right up ahead, on the right. Keep your eyes open, guys. Ranger says we should be able to spot it from the road even though it's not paved."

"Hey! That's Ranger's truck. Why is he out here?"

The truck was on the side of the road, but there was no sign of Ranger. Josh said, "Just pull in behind him. Given his condition, I can guarantee he's somewhere nearby. Why would he come back down here?"

I slid the SUV in behind the truck, and just a few seconds later Pete and Sara pulled in behind us. *Ease up, Midas. It's over. Looks like you're the odd man out.*

"Geesh," Sierra whispered behind me, "what a lot of nerve."

"Come on, guys. We have a job to do. Let's find Ranger and get started on this investigation. No drama."

"You got it, boss." Josh hopped out and grabbed a small duffel bag. He and Sierra didn't waste any time sorting through the electronics.

I popped the back and waved Cassidy over. "You ready to jump in with both feet?"

"I'm game. What cha got for me?"

"This is called a K2 meter. It lets us know if there are fluctuations in the electromagnetic field." I switched on the device and pointed at the green light. "When things are normal, you'll see the green light. If there are changes detected, the light will bounce up to orange and even red. I've got some that also give off a digital reading, but I think this will work for now. Get you acclimated to the equipment. When we walk in, we'll sweep around and get a feel for the place. Some places naturally have an elevated field, and if that's the case here, we want to know about it. How are you feeling, Cassidy?"

"I'm wondering what the hell I'm doing traipsing around the woods with a group of ghost hunters."

I cracked another smile. "I can see why you'd be asking yourself that. But just a word of caution, these guys prefer to be called paranormal investigators."

With wide eyes she said, "I'm glad you warned me. Okay, so we wait fifteen minutes and go in, or do we look for Mr. Shaw first?"

The GCP team gathered around me and waited to hear my answer. "Josh and Sierra will go in first. Pete and Sara will follow after fifteen, and then we'll go in. That will give Cassidy and me time to look around for Ranger. How's that sound?"

"Fine with me," Sara said with a sweet smile. "Let's take a look at that map again. If I remember correctly, there's an abandoned barn around here somewhere. I marked it up on the small map. Come on, Cassidy. I'll give you a crash course in map reading."

Cassidy followed Sara to her white sedan. Pete didn't stick around; he jogged down the side of the road to check in the nearest ditch for any sign of Ranger. Sierra eyeballed me as she cracked her gum. "You think that's a good idea?"

I shut the back and frowned at her. "I'm not worried about Cassidy...she can handle herself. And you need to get a life, Little Sister." She was very much like a little sister to me, so much so that I was willing to kick Josh's ass if need be. Sierra had a big heart, too big at times, and she often said things most of us were already thinking but were too polite to say. Sometimes I had to rein her in.

"Roger that, captain." She clicked the stopwatch on her phone. "See you in thirty minutes. Turn your walkie on and quit staring at the Doublemint Twins."

"What? They are hardly twins."

"Whatever. Bye."

Sierra and Josh left holding hands. I joined Pete in the search for Ranger. I hoped he man was okay.

Chapter Twelve—Cassidy

"Sierra to base."

Sara's well-manicured nails wrapped around the black walkie-talkie. "This is base. Go ahead, Sierra."

"Five minutes. No sign of the client. K2 is even Steven. Temp is 58F."

"Great. Check back in five. Radio silence, please."

"All right."

She tapped the antenna of the walkie-talkie to her chin. "I hope she remembers to take pictures. Did she take her camera?" she asked Midas. It was the first time she'd spoken to him this afternoon.

"Yes, but it wouldn't hurt to have a backup. You have yours?"

Sara cocked an eyebrow at him. "Are you kidding? I'm no rookie." She cast a stinging look of disdain in my direction and strolled back to her car in her stylish brown boots and began searching her backseat, presumably for her camera.

"Am I missing something?" I couldn't help but ask. The uncomfortable feeling kept rising. I'd had enough weirdness for one day.

Nobody answered me. Midas glared after Sara, but it was Peter who broke the silence.

"Cassidy, have you always been interested in the supernatural? Seems like we all have our own stories to tell. All of us have either seen something or lost someone. They say the loss of a loved one in a tragic way makes you more sensitive to the spirit world. I think that might be true."

"You're an ass, Pete. You're joking about her sister? She doesn't know she's lost her." I could see Midas' muscles ripple under his shirt. He wore a navy blue sweater, the thin, fitted kind that had three buttons at the top.

"I'm sorry, Cassidy. I swear to you I'm not a heartless beast."

"How could you not know?" Sara scolded him. "She told us about her the other night."

"I had my headphones on half the time, cueing up video and photographs. Shoot. I'm really sorry, Cassie."

That was the last straw. I was about to tell him how I really felt about his "joke." I took a deep breath and said, "My name is Cassidy, and…"

The walkie-talkie squawked, and I heard Sierra's voice, "Hey! Y'all need to get in here, now!"

Immediately everyone began running toward the narrow pathway. Midas snatched the walkie. "Sierra! What's up!"

"Someone's out here — stalking us."

"Can you see who it is? Is it Ranger?"

"Definitely not! Footsteps are too fast for someone so sick." Her whisper sent a shiver down my spine. "I'm taking pictures…should we keep pushing in toward the house?"

"Yes, keep going. We're double-timing your way. Stay on the path, Sierra. Don't get lost. Follow your GPS. It should lead you right to it."

"Okay."

"Midas! Let's flank whoever this is!" Pete said, his anger rising.

Midas looked at me as if to say, "Are you going to be all right?"

Sara said, "Go and help Sierra. Cassidy and I will follow."

Immediately Midas took off to the left and Peter to the right. They flanked the narrow road and scurried through the woods to see if they could detect the intruder.

Sara handed me her audio recorder. "Hold this! I'm grabbing some photos. We're going to run, Cassidy. I hope you can keep up."

"Sure, I used to run marathons." I didn't want to seem like a wimp. Now didn't seem like the time to tell her that I hadn't trained in over six months. "But why are we running? Are they in danger, do you think? Maybe it's just a homeless person."

"The element of surprise! Hit record and come on! Get your ass in gear, girl!"

I pressed the record button, gritted my teeth and took off after her. We ran down the leaf-littered path; the afternoon sunlight was casting lean shadows in a few spots now. We'd be out of sun soon. Then we'd be running through the woods in the dark. Was it supposed to be this cold out here?

I wish I held the temperature thingy instead, but I didn't.

"You feel that, Cassidy? The cold?" She bounded over a log in front of me, and I followed her. "Not unusual for the woods, but this is more than that," she said breathlessly. "I think it might mean we've got supernatural activity out here."

"You think?" I asked sincerely.

She paused her running. Her pretty cheeks were pink and healthy-looking. She'd worn her long hair in a ponytail today, and she wore blue jeans that fit her perfectly.

"Yeah, I do. I think it's time you get your feet wet, rookie. Use the audio recorder. Ask a few questions."

"Um, what? What kind of questions?"

"Ask a question like, 'Are there any spirits around me that want to talk?'"

I repeated what she said. I spun around slowly and looked around the forest, but there wasn't a sound. Not even bird sounds or a squirrel rattling through the leaves. And it didn't just sound dead; it felt dead.

"Do you feel that, Cassidy?"

"Yes. It feels…empty."

"That's what you want on an investigation. If the place is empty of living things, that means other things are near. Keep talking."

I shivered at her words. "Are you Aurelia Davis, the wife of Bernard? If so, what are you doing out here?" I watched the K2 going wild. Sara gave me a thumbs-up and began snapping photos like a fiend. I kept going. "Are you Cope, Bernard Davis' slave?" I thought I heard a whisper, so I kept going. "What are you doing here?"

The audio recorder began to beep. "Oh my God! You got something, Cassidy!" The walkie-talkie squawked again.

"We're okay. Where are you guys?"

"We'll be there in a minute."

I followed Sara, unbelieving that I had actually caught something.

When we reached the group, I was out of breath. A clear sign that I'd let myself go too long without proper exercise. The sun hadn't set yet, but purple shadows were edging up from the ground. Sierra said, "So he was here, but I don't see any footprints. Josh, you got your flashlight, sweetie?" She accepted a mini flashlight from Joshua and began searching the ground. "Someone was definitely here, though. Lots of leaves."

"Yeah, I'm not seeing any footprints over here either."

"Tell me what this guy was doing. Was he threatening you? Did he have a weapon?" Midas stood with one hand on his chin and the other on his hip as he listened to Joshua relate their encounter.

"Sierra thought she heard someone, and we called out a few times thinking maybe it was Ranger out here, but he never answered. Whoever he was, he got real still and didn't come out in the open. I could only see his outline a few times. He stayed behind the trees there, but the strange-ass thing was he ran from that side to this side and we don't know how he did it."

"Did you take some photos, Sierra?" Sara asked as she flipped through her own drive.

"Yes, mother," Sierra said sarcastically, "but I got nothing to show for it." She skimmed through the pictures with a frustrated expression. "I'll have to take another look back at HQ."

Midas broke out his flashlight. "Let's do one more sweep for footprints, and then we'll review the photos together back at home base. You know you can't see much on those tiny screens. You guys see any rubbish that might indicate we're in someone's camp?"

Peter said, "I saw one Wal-Mart bag tied to a tree on the road. That means there's at least one homeless person back here — or there was once."

"Okay, use caution. If you see..." Midas was speaking, but I wasn't listening. I heard something, something the others hadn't heard yet. It was the sound of an owl.

"Shh...you hear that?"

Everyone got still. We instinctively made a circle, each of us looking around for whatever might be approaching. I heard the sound again, but it was further away now. It was definitely an owl.

"Was that an owl?" Sierra asked me.

"I think so. But it sounds like a regular, living owl, not Aurelia's demon-bird."

"Shoot," Sierra said. "Well, maybe Josh and I should head in that direction?"

Midas nodded, and the two traveled north. "I want to go this way," I said to Sara. "Want to take a walk?"

Sara shrugged. "Sure, whatever you think." Midas didn't stop us; he and Peter continued searching for whoever it was that Sierra and Joshua encountered.

Cassidy...

"Did you call my name, Sara?"

"No, but I heard a whisper." We both got very still, like two redheaded statues in a forgotten forest.

I heard nothing else and whispered to Sara, "It's this way."

"What's this way? What are we looking for?"

I didn't answer her. The compulsion had me in its clutches—the same compulsion I'd felt when I painted the portrait of Aurelia Davis. In fact, I felt it so strongly that I could hardly breathe. I began to run, forgetting about the cramps in my side and the investigator who trailed behind me. I wasn't far from it now. Just one more fence, another copse of trees, another hillside...I could hear Sara calling my name, but I couldn't answer her. I was a moth, and this place, Oak Grove, was the flame. I had to go. I had to see. I had to know.

Soon the only thing separating me from the house was a rusty wire fence. I could easily climb this thing or poke my way through it. But as I put my leg through I heard another voice say, "Go back!" Surprised, I fell back on the ground. Suddenly, towering over me on the opposite side of the fence was a black shadow with no face. But it wasn't just any shadow, it was a familiar one. It was Cope!

"Go back!" he growled at me. Then he vanished like someone had turned out the light. I stared at the shimmering air, unable to move.

"Cassidy! You can't run off like that, girl. What if you'd gotten hurt out here? That's not how a paranormal investigator works on this team. We don't take off into the woods to...oh my God! Is that the plantation? I had no idea we were so close. You could have just said something."

"Yes. That's it," I said as I got up off the ground. I shook leaves off my sweater and waited. She began to snap photos of the house.

"Wow, that's some neat place. I imagine with the original wings on the house it was something to see. A pretty country jewel." Click, click, click.

"Oh, no. It was never that."

"Hey! Cassidy, come here. Do you see that guy? Who is that standing on the porch? Man, he's tall. Probably seven feet tall. That has to be an illusion. I wonder if he knows who owns the house..." She scrunched her brows and then had an idea. "Sir! Hey! Can we talk to you a second?"

He didn't move. It was plainly a black man in a ragged t-shirt and blue pants. He looked out of place, and that was putting it mildly. And then I heard the voice again, although his mouth didn't move. "Get out...leave here."

That man was the shadow that met me at the fence and disappeared! That man wasn't a man, he was a ghost!

"Hey, mister!" Sara kept calling to him. She was looking for a way through the fence.

"Sara," I said, putting my hand on her shoulder, "that's not who you think it is. That's a..." And as soon as I began to speak the words, the man vanished. He didn't fade away, he didn't run away. He vanished. And he didn't want us here.

And I alone knew what it was we were dealing with. It was the man Aurelia cared for so much, the one she'd asked to kill her, to deliver her to death so she could escape the daily pain at Bernard's hands. I was wrong when I believed he was chasing Aurelia through the woods.

He wasn't chasing her, he was protecting her. And from the looks of it, he protected her to this day.

And we were not wanted here.

Chapter Thirteen—Cassidy

I blew off the team meeting. I gave Sierra a quick interview, so they'd have my testimony on record, and also handed over the audio files and all the equipment I'd handled. These guys dotted their I's and crossed their T's, that was for sure. Each item had to be signed back in and charged up.

I felt tired, more tired than I had in a long time. I needed to hide now. Away from people, away from the supernatural. I needed to be normal and do normal things, like empty my dishwasher, have the locks changed and sweep my dusty floors. I needed to do those things, not chase ghosts, at least for a few hours. When it was all said and done, when the dishwasher was unloaded and I'd worked on a clothing stain for ten minutes and the garbage had been taken out, I felt better. I loved my loft. It was my sanctuary. The wide open spaces worked for me. I loved the bare windows and the sparse furniture. I didn't need a lot of things. Just a comfortable bed and a decent desk chair. And plenty of easels.

I toyed with the idea of looking up some of those black owls online, but it was eight o'clock and I was yawning nonstop. I decided to put an end to my day. Since the locksmith couldn't come until tomorrow, I slid a chair under the door to keep Mike out and flopped down on my down comforter — so nice to be in my bed. Never had I been so happy to be in my soft pajamas. An alert on my phone let me know I had a message.

Please don't be from Mike.

It wasn't. It was Midas. I smiled a big, silly smile. I was glad he couldn't see me. He was so intense-looking; his dark eyes were always searching, like he wanted to know every secret I had. And his smiles were so rare. I'd seen them only a few times since I'd known him.

You did great today. Are you ready to quit yet?

Nope. I'm ready to get to the bottom of this. Why is Cope still protecting Aurelia? Doesn't he know she's gone?

You'll have your chance to ask him tomorrow night. We are headed to the house at 6 pm for a lights-out, full-on investigation. Want to have lunch tomorrow?

Demeter's? LOL

No. I have something else in mind. Pick you up at 11?

See you then. Should I wear hiking boots? It was a joke, so I wasn't expecting his answer.

Yes. And long sleeves. Night, Cassidy.

Night, Midas.

And I did sleep, and for the first time in a hundred forevers, I dreamed about Kylie Starr. Mom was holding her. Mom's long blond hair was sticking to her chest. She was all sweaty; she'd worked so hard to have Kylie. We were at the hospital. No, this wasn't a dream but a memory. Dad was there too, smiling from ear to ear. I sat on the pleather couch in Mom's hospital room. Dad leaned down, his red hair falling into his eyes. With a smile he said to me, "Watch your sister, Cassidy. Don't take your eyes off her, okay?" I nodded in my dream, and suddenly the room changed. It kind of swirled about; I was still sitting on the couch, but I was in a different place.

We were at the funeral home. Mom had died in the hospital, something about complications, and I held Kylie in my lap while Dad spoke to everyone quietly.

Then the dream changed again. We were at home, on the blue couch, and I could hear Uncle Derek and Dad arguing. I held my sister and gave her a bottle. She was my baby now. I must take care of her.

Shh…baby Kylie. Don't fuss so. It's all right. I'm here. Cassidy is here.

I tuned out Uncle Derek and Dad and focused on the baby in my arms. I sang to her all the songs that Mom had sung to me. Kylie made sweet noises under her blanket like she couldn't get enough of that bottle, but then the sounds changed. No, she changed! I could feel the change too.

She was changing in my lap, moving, scratching — growing! I decided I had to pull back the covers. I had to see her face. I had to know that she was still Kylie. With my young hands shaking, I touched the top of the blanket and stared down at Kylie while I uncovered her. It was not Kylie!

I was holding a bird, a black bird — a black owl! It began to tear at my flesh with its evil talons and pecked at me with its beak. "Kylie! No! Daddy! Help me!"

Daddy swirled away and was gone. Kylie had been stolen, replaced by the evil owl. Suddenly the thing flew away; one talon scratched into my shoulder, and then it was gone.

I woke up screaming and praying. "Kylie!" I swung the blanket off me and looked around for evidence of Kylie or the bird. There was no evidence of either.

Except for the long scratch on my shoulder.

The pain was blinding and I sat on the edge of the bed, the wound screaming. The bird had been here. And that meant somehow, Kylie had been here. And if she was here, she must be dead. I didn't want to believe it. I couldn't believe it.

I sat on the floor, bleeding and crying. In between nervous looks around my loft and crying jags, I called the only person I knew who would believe me. I called Midas. Forget about it being "too soon" and all. I blubbered into the phone and hardly made any sense at all. He didn't wait for further explanation.

"I'm on the way."

I lay on the floor and cried like it was the day Kylie disappeared.

Chapter Fourteen—*Midas*

Rubbing my eyes, I got dressed in the dark. By the tone of Cassidy's voice, there was something going on at her apartment. And for some reason, I needed to be there. I had to make sure she was all right. But there was no sense in waking up my house guest.

Sara had called me little more than three hours ago and wanted to come over and talk. I welcomed that idea, but her idea of talking was to get me into bed. So was I wrong about her and Peter?

"Come on, Midas. Just for old times' sake." For the first time in our relationship, I didn't say yes.

"I want to be friends, Sara. Not friends with benefits, or however that goes."

Sara stood on her tiptoes, kicked off her stiletto heels and wrapped her slender arms around my neck. "There is nothing going on between Peter and me. If that's what you're thinking."

"If I'm thinking that, you led me to believe it."

She shrugged and didn't deny it. "We just have mutual interests, that's all."

"You mean you, right?" I said, playing along. I had to admit the soft feel of her sweater dress was delicious beneath my hands. That was a good word to describe sex with Sara: delicious. But anything beyond that? Nope. Nothing nice about her at all.

She'd changed, that was for sure. Besides, she was leaving in a few weeks. This was a game to her.

"Friends, Sara. We're friends." I eased her slender arms gently off my neck. "I hope you understand that."

"Whatever, Midas. You're being such a jerk." Sara crossed her arms and sighed. "Well, I brought this bottle of wine with me. I plan on drinking it. You want some?"

"No. I'm reviewing these photos. You want to see?"

"No, I don't need to see the photos. I was there, re-member?"

"You never did tell me what you saw, Sara. At Oak Grove. I'd like to get the details of your observation. Use this device." She shook her head and refused to hold it. She was too busy pulling the cork out of her bottle.

"I don't want to talk about ghosts, Midas. I'm not like you. I don't need to do this 24-7." She sighed as she poured the wine into a glass.

"All right, I'll have a glass of wine with you." I slid the recorder in my pocket. Maybe she was right.

She must have changed her mind because she began talking in a low, thoughtful tone. "The newbie, Cas-sidy, she took off running, and I followed her. I think she knew where she was going from the be-ginning. Like she'd already been there, scouting out the place. Or at least some part of her knew. I ran after her, and when I caught up to her she was sitting on the ground, looking up at the fence."

"Did she run into the fence?"

"I'm sure she didn't. Something frightened her. You heard her testimony. She told it exactly as it happened."

"Yes, but what did you see, Sara?"

She curled up on my couch and tossed a blanket over her legs. A fire roared in the fireplace, but neither of us paid much attention to it.

"Believe it or not, I saw a ghost. Yes, me, Miss Sensible Skeptic. He was a black man; he looked poor and unusually tall. He didn't want us there; I could see that—I could feel it. I was glad to leave when we did. He just vanished, like someone switched off a light. One minute he was there, and the next he was gone. I got the feeling he's guarding that house or something."

"Cassidy says he's guarding Aurelia. He must not understand that she's dead."

"Well, it sounds like you should help him understand that. I'm not looking forward to going back to Kali Oka Road, but I bet you are, aren't you?"

I stared at the fire and said, "What do you think? Of course I want to go back there. And I got permission to tour Oak Grove too."

"I never doubted you, Midas. You can be charming when you want to be." She twisted a curl with a finger and took another gulp. "It's going to be scary as hell going in that house, now that I know there is something really there. Imagine, my last investigation with GCP, and I'm finally convinced that there is a spiritual world."

"Come on, Sara. You were sure there was something at the Bowery. And what about the yacht club? You saw a shadow figure there."

"I'm not sure what I saw, not a hundred percent. But at Oak Grove, there was no denying he was there. He stared at us like he hated us. Like he'd hurt us if we tried to come in."

"Interesting. I hope this is an actual haunt and not something else. The owl creature is a disturbing twist to this case."

"Did you ever get a hold of Ranger? Find out where he went and what he was doing out there?"

"Nope, I haven't. I called him; I hope the guy is okay. I left a message on his voicemail. If he doesn't call me back by noon tomorrow, I'll check with his son."

This conversation was strange. Yesterday I was convinced Sara would hate me forever. Now it was like we were friends again, chatting about the latest investigation. I couldn't understand why it couldn't stay like this. But we were past that now.

She sipped her wine and said thoughtfully, "If there was a way you could show the ghost Aurelia's grave or let him know she's gone, maybe you could help him find rest. But then again, it is possible we aren't working on the right narrative. Can we be so sure that Cassidy knows what she's talking about? There's every chance that she's just a disturbed girl who's obsessed with the place."

"Her sister's disappearance is real. I checked it out. She's not making that up. I don't think she's making up what she sees either."

"I leave you to it, then. Work your magic, Midas. Rescue the damsel in distress. You were always good at it. I just don't need rescuing anymore." I couldn't help myself. I touched her soft hair and toyed with a curl.

"I'm going to miss this. I enjoyed these times, talking to you about things."

"Talking about the supernatural, you mean. Never about our future, or kids, or anything beyond Gulf Coast Paranormal. You talk about it constantly. Can you understand that a girl needs more sometimes, Midas? I admit your handsome face makes it hard to leave, but I have to go. I have to see what's beyond the next door. And your first love will always be the next investigation."

I couldn't help but laugh. "Are you kidding me? You're the one with the contract to appear on a reality television show about paranormal investigations. But you say I'm the one obsessed with ghosts."

"I'm going to do what I always wanted to do, and that's act. I love it. Once I leave GCP, all my investigations will be fully scripted." She raised her glass as if she wanted to make a toast to herself. "Don't look at me like that. I'm not a sellout. I'm doing what's best for me. You had a chance to bring this whole thing to the big screen, and you didn't want it. Remember?"

"Sure, I remember. Peter is still ticked about it."

Then it got quiet. I stayed on my side of the couch even though my body had other ideas. If it was over, it was over. If I wanted to keep Sara with me, I'd have to marry her. And no matter how I played that out in my mind, that was a marriage that wouldn't work. Probably because for the first time ever I had to admit that I didn't love her. Not like a man needs to love the woman he marries. I enjoyed her, respected her, and appreciated her. Liked her. Loved things *about* her, but I didn't love her.

And she knew it.

She was doing the best thing for herself. I wasn't going to stop her. "I think you should tell the team tomorrow so they can celebrate with you. It's a step up, Sara. You do what's right for you. We'll be fine."

She sipped more of the wine and giggled. "I'm sure you will. If a certain fellow redhead has anything to say about it."

"We've only known each other a couple of days."

"She needs you. You like it when they need you. Maybe that was the problem with us, Midas. I just didn't need you enough. Not like that."

"Stop talking like that. Let's stay in touch, Sara. Not just say it. Let's do it."

"If you think we can, I'm for it. I'm sorry I was such a witch to you earlier. I do want to be friends again." She finished her glass, and I poured her another one. "Hey, can I crash here tonight? I don't think I want to drive. Imagine…I finally break into Hollywood but can't go to the first filming because I've been arrested for DUI. Wouldn't that be peachy?"

From there our conversation went to her new job as a lead actress on her hot new show. She revealed the pay she was offered, and it was staggering. We talked about her getting an apartment in LA somewhere. She had a cousin, Serenity, out there. I thought that was the perfect California name. She'd agreed to let Sara stay for the first six months until she could get everything together. After a while, Sara hunkered down on the couch, and I covered her with a blanket and kissed her forehead. "Night, Sara."

"Night, Midas. I'm going to miss you."

"I'll miss you too." I clicked off the light and went to my bedroom. I didn't bother changing my clothes. My brain didn't allow me to sleep. Not yet. I had to toss around the various factors of our current case. And of course, I thought about Cassidy. I didn't know why I was so drawn to her...it wasn't like I had a specific thing for redheads. And it wasn't because she had a vague resemblance to Sara. There was something else for sure. Why was I thinking about her? Was it because everyone else was assuming that I was romantically interested in her? Finally, I felt tired and was able to close my eyes. I didn't dream, but then I rarely did. When my phone rang, the sound startled me.

"Yeah? Hello?"

"Midas...there's this bird..." It was Cassidy. She was crying and sounded frightened. I immediately flung the covers off and sat up. She continued, "I think I'm bleeding."

I told her I was on the way and got dressed as quickly as possible.

I had every intention of tiptoeing out of the apartment, and I would have cleared it if I hadn't stubbed my toe on a dining room chair. I swore silently, but it didn't matter. Sara heard me and got up off the couch.

"So now who's up for a booty call? Or a midnight snack."

"No booties are calling, Sara. Go back to sleep."

"Okay, I will if you'll stop banging the furniture around."

"Good night, Sara."

"Good night, Midas." She lay back down, flipped her back to me and covered up with the blanket.

I left as quietly as I could.

Chapter Fifteen—Cassidy

I slid the chair out from under the door and let Midas in. "What happened? Was it Mike again?"

"If it was Mike, I wouldn't be calling you. It was the bird. The owl, I mean. It was here." I carefully made my way to the nearest kitchen table chair.

"Wait, where are your towels?"

I nodded toward the kitchen linen drawer. "In there. And there's a first aid kit under the sink. I haven't even looked at this thing yet, but it feels like a pterodactyl got a hold of me."

Midas grabbed everything he needed and returned with a grim look on his face. "I need you to lift your shirt so I can see it." He slid on plastic gloves from the kit and waited.

"Close your eyes for a sec." He did as I asked and after a few seconds I said, "Okay, you can open them." I clutched my shirt to my chest and gritted my teeth as he began probing the area with his gloved finger. I couldn't look him in the eye. This was all too weird. Midas moved my hair out of the way so he could get a better view of the cut.

"I think you might need stitches, Cassidy." He began blotting the blood away.

"I hope not. I hate needles. Ow! Shoot! That hurts. Is it real bad?" I twisted around like a kid who wanted to see the injury but was afraid to look at it.

"Bad enough to need a few stitches, I think. Be still and I'll try to stop the bleeding. What happened?"

"Look, I know it's late and this is a huge imposition, but I swear it was that owl. The one from the painting — Ranger's owl."

He didn't say anything for a minute, just cleaned the wound and applied four or five bandages along with some antibiotic cream. I began to feel like I'd done the wrong thing. During Mike's short stay here, he'd installed a mirror over the kitchen sink. Did I mention he liked looking at himself? I could see Midas clearly in the mirror, his furrowed brow, his serious expression. "Midas? Did you hear me? I'm sorry I called this late."

"No need to apologize, Cassidy. I'm sorry this happened. Who's to say me involving you in this case hasn't stirred up something here?" He glanced around the loft as if he were in a ghost-detecting mood. "Tell me exactly what happened."

"Well, it started with a dream about Kylie. I was back at the hospital the day she was born. I was holding her when my Mom died. Dad told me to watch her, that actually happened. But then the scene changed a few times. Hold on a second. I'm going to go grab a shirt if you don't mind. I'll be right back." I padded to my bedroom and rummaged for a large t-shirt. I cringed a little as I pulled it over my head, but I didn't waste time hanging around. My bedroom didn't feel safe anymore. I didn't want to be in here.

Back in my kitchen, Midas was tidying up the mess. I sat back down in the chair and pulled my knees up, wrapping my arms around them.

"You said the scene changed a few times?"

"Yes, I was at the hospital and then a few other places, and the whole time I had this bundle in my arms. I thought it was Kylie. Then it wasn't Kylie, it was that owl! I was holding it in the blanket, but it got out. It scared the hell out of me! I woke up, and the thing was still in my room, flying over me. It scratched me and then vanished."

Midas pursed his lips as he listened. With a nod, he said, "Show me where you were."

"Okay." I tucked my hair behind my ears and went back to the bedroom. I turned on the light this time because that feeling of dread hadn't yet disappeared. "I sleep on the left side. That's where I was." I noticed a few drops of blood on my sheets, probably from where the thing had scratched me.

"Do you mind?" He wanted to check out my bed.

"No, go ahead."

He lay down where I usually lay and put his hands behind his head. I tried not to stare at his muscular body or imagine what it would be like to snuggle up next to him. I glanced around at the corners of the ceiling and didn't find whatever it was he was looking for. He sat on the side of the bed and began looking behind my pillows and under my bed. If he asked to search my nightstand, I'd have to draw the line.

"What are you expecting to find?"

"Rule number one in paranormal investigation, Cassidy. Always make an attempt to debunk. Always. Even if the person who reports the event is someone you know. I want to help you, but this is how I work."

"I can assure you there is no scientific explanation for an owl in my dream coming through my dream and attacking me in real life."

He patted the bed and walked to the window. It was closed tight. I never opened my bedroom window. I never even opened the blinds. "Don't be defensive. It's possible to have dreams morph as you wake up. Have you ever heard of night terrors? Or sleep paralysis?"

"Sure, but it wasn't sleep paralysis."

"How can you be so sure?"

"Because I could move just fine. Or else that demon-bird would have ripped me to shreds."

"Well, during sleep paralysis, the brain wakes up before the body does. And when that happens," Midas said as he continued to tug at the window, "the brain presents us with images to explain the phenomenon. But you're right, this doesn't sound like sleep paralysis. So let's think like investigators. What else could it be? Let's rule some things out before we call this a paranormal event. It might be, but we can't say for sure yet."

I knew what I saw, but I liked the idea of detaching myself from the weird experience. "All right. Let me think. The creature was in the room. If I were a skeptic, I would say look for an open window or some other point of entry."

"Good. Let's check the windows."

I didn't for a minute think this thing was a figment of my imagination, nor did I believe it was a friend-ly hoot owl that got lost and decided to hide in my apartment. However, this exercise did make me feel better. We searched the apartment and found only one window open—the kitchen window. "I swear I shut that thing this morning. And yesterday I found it open too. What could be opening this window?" Then the answered occurred to me. "Mike?"

Midas peered out the window but didn't spot any birds, certainly not any large owls. He closed it and flipped the lock shut. He tried to pull the window up, but the lock held tight. "This is a puzzler. Could your ex-roommate have more than one key?"

"I had the locks changed. I'm the only one with a key now." I rubbed my lip furiously; the scratch on my back reminded me that it was there.

"So potentially this could be a bird. I saw birdseed on the balcony. Do you feed birds out there?"

I sighed and sat back down at the kitchen table, suddenly feeling very embarrassed. "Not anymore. My neighbor complained about it and I had to quit."

"So it's possible that a bird was out there and flew through the window. You woke up, half asleep, the bird attacked you, and you naturally thought it was the owl." He sat next to me and looked me in the eye. "Cassidy, if the Kali Oka Road investigation is too much for you, if it's disturbing you at this level, you don't have to participate. Maybe my invitation set things off for you."

"Are you saying you don't want me to participate in the investigation now? How will that help me?"

He covered my hand with his big one. His skin felt warm and reassuring. He didn't hold my hand long, but it was long enough for me to know that he cared. Or was concerned. Or something.

"All right, can we use your computer? Let's talk to Sierra."

"It's kind of late. Do you think she's up?" I glanced at the clock but led him to my computer desk anyway.

"She's up."

"Sure, it's over here."

He grabbed another chair and sat next to me at the desk. He clicked an icon, and the computer began ringing. After a few seconds, Sierra's pretty face popped up on the screen. "Midas? Where are you calling from? Oh. Never mind. Hi, Cassidy. Geesh, you look like heck."

"I'm at Cassidy's place. We need your help with something. Cassidy was attacked tonight, by a bird."

"No kidding?"

"I think it was the owl, but I'm not absolutely sure. Tell us what you know about Aurelia's demon-bird. Could this be some kind of manifestation?" Cassidy leaned forward anxiously.

Sierra snatched her hair into a ponytail and tossed a jellybean in her mouth. "Okay, let me open the file. I actually found quite a few things. Hey, Josh! Guess who I'm talking to?" she shouted over her shoulder. Joshua popped in rubbing his eyes.

"Hey, Midas. And Cassidy. Got to take a shower. I got to get up early. My old man needs me at the laundry. Later, guys."

Sierra frowned at his back and rolled her eyes. "Anyway…here. I've got it. Let's see. I think it's better that I read this.

"Oral traditions in most American tribes associate owls with death warnings, and an owl is typically the bearer of the deceased's soul as it passes from this world to the next. Cherokee women bathed their children's eyes in water containing owl feathers, believing it would help them stay awake during ominous nights. This Cherokee tale explains why owls are nocturnal:

"When the animals and plants were first made — we do not know by whom — they were told to watch and keep awake for seven nights, just as young men now fast and keep awake during their medicine trials. They tried to do this, and nearly all were awake through the first night, but the next night several dropped off to sleep, and the third night others were asleep, and then others, until on the seventh night, of all the animals only the owl, the panther and one or two more were still awake. To these were given the power to see and to go about in the dark, and to make prey of the birds and animals that must sleep at night."

"That's interesting and all, but what about local legends?" I asked impatiently. The cuts on my back were screaming now. Maybe Midas was right that I needed stitches.

"All in all, there are four or five 'ghost' reports from that area, and only a few reports of Ranger's black owl. The first, most prominent report is associated with a tall, black man, a slave who was killed at the house for some crime against the Davis family. Horrible death, too. They say he was chained to the oak tree, one of the large ones at the front of the property, chained but cut up enough to bleed out. After he died, the plantation owner left him hanging there until he rotted. Supposedly this was a warning to the plantation owner's wife, who'd taken a fancy to the slave. People see him a lot, sometimes on the porch, sometimes in the woods."

"Gross," I said with a shiver. "What else?"

"The next is the Lady in White, which I suppose we could assume is Aurelia Davis. She's looking for either the man or the baby. Rumor has it that she had a baby who wasn't her husband's. The husband tossed the baby off the bridge—that's where the legend of Crybaby Bridge began. That's one iteration of it. She's also seen in the cemetery, around the tree, and in the forest."

My mind raced back to the painting and what I saw as Aurelia.

"What else?" Midas asked.

"Besides a few ghost lights, which are common near the cemetery and the road, you might also see the haint."

"What the heck is a haint? I'm afraid to ask," I said. Sierra appeared genuinely amused.

"A haint can be different things, depending on which region of the south you are in. In this area and during the time in question, a haint was a kind of witch, a gypsy who wandered the counties offering her services to the highest bidder. Only this haint got her hooks into one wealthy customer, Bernard Davis."

"What kind of services did she offer him?" Midas asked suspiciously.

"She'd curse his enemies, sic a demon on them, cast spells on his behalf. Mr. Davis' friend's name has been lost over the years. Apparently the haint, whoever she was, lived on his property and was frequently summoned to the plantation for consultation. Mr. Davis was a man who believed in the supernatural."

"And where do you get that from?"

"This really interesting memoir from R. L. Pettway. He lived in the county and was a careful writer. His journals have a ton of information about the time in question. He says that Davis was a hard man, both in his words and in his propensity for cruelty toward animals and people he disagreed with, which was most everyone. Pettway sold Davis a horse once and never saw it again. For some reason, he got the idea that Davis bought the horse just to kill it. His journal says he deeply regretted selling that horse to Davis. He writes that when he complained about the horse's disappearance, the haint sent the owl to his house. It flew in the window, tore up his pet cat, scratched him all up and was gone."

"That's incredible!" I could well believe that story. Bernard had to have been horrible if his wife was so fearful of him.

Midas said, "Pretty strange. Even if that were true, say Davis did have a pet owl, how in the world would it live this long? Maybe this owl is a spirit animal of some kind."

The three of us sat in silence as Sierra shared images she'd found online, supposedly of this bird. None looked like the bird I'd seen, but some were close. "Why would the owl thing visit me? And why would it pretend to be Kylie?"

"Maybe the haint sent it?" Sierra joked. Joshua walked back through the camera view with a towel wrapped around his waist. "Hmm...I think I'd better go. I'll catch you in the morning, Midas. You'll send us the details about tomorrow night's investigation? I hope we find answers."

"I'll call you in the morning. Good night, Sierra." Midas got up to answer a phone call. I tried not to listen.

Sierra grinned at me. "So you two?"

"There's nothing going on, Sierra. I swear that bird came here. It came after me—it scratched up my back."

"Mm hmm..." she said sweetly. Then she whispered, "Well, I'm just glad he's not with Sara. Gotta go!" She closed her computer, and the screen went blank.

Midas came back and peered at me. "You going to be all right by yourself?"

"Sure. What you said made sense. It probably was a bird that got in here, got scared and then scratched me. I'll go see the doctor in the morning, make sure I'm up to date on my tetanus shot. Sorry I was such a baby."

"I didn't mean that. I don't mind at all. It's just that I have someone at the house."

"Sara," I said, sounding disappointed.

"Well, yeah. But it's not what you might think."

I walked to the door to show him out. "I don't think anything. And it's none of my business. Please tell her I'm sorry that I interrupted your...time together. Thanks for coming."

With an awkward nod, he left the apartment. I closed the door and leaned against it until my back reminded me that I had a significant wound there.

"What's the matter with you, Cassidy? You act like a complete mess around this man." I promised myself I was going to stop acting like a fool every time I was in his presence. He was clearly spoken for, and I wasn't interested in him anyway, was I?

I changed the sheets and pillowcases on my bed, as if that would help to erase my earlier experience. I made sure the windows were closed and slid back into bed. It was hard to get comfortable, and not just because of the cuts. I had the feeling that someone was watching me. I turned the bedside light on and eventually closed my eyes. I must have fallen asleep because the next thing I knew, the sun was streaming in from the other room.

Chapter Sixteen—*Midas*

"Ranger, when you get this message, please call me. I have some information about your case."

Less than a minute later, I did get a call. But it wasn't from Ranger Shaw; it was from Richard Harlen, the man who currently owned Oak Grove Plantation. The house had passed through quite a few hands during its lifetime and had been neglected for many of those years, but Mr. Harlen had every intention of restoring the old place. At least that's what I'd heard.

"Good morning. Is this Midas Demopolis?"

"Yes, it is. Mr. Harlen?"

"Call me Junior. I got your message. My daughter tells me you are interested in my house? I'm going out there this morning. Supposed to meet the contractor who's going to help me restore the place. If you'd like to come out, Barbara and I would be glad to talk to you."

"Thank you, Junior. What time?"

"I'm headed that way now. How about 8:30?"

"That sounds great. I'm on the way. Thanks in advance." I hung up the phone and quickly made my way to the shower. Sara had left early; the only evidence that she'd been here was an empty wine glass and a folded blanket on the couch. I paused in the doorway wondering what that had been all about. Hopefully whatever had been wrong was now right. I could never tell with Sara.

I opted for blue jeans and a long-sleeved shirt. If Mr. Harlen really did give me access to the house, I wanted to be prepared. I grabbed batteries for the camera and the EMF detector, and then I headed out the door.

As I slung the items into the passenger seat of the car, I called Peter. He had mentioned some new technology he wanted to try on our next investigation, a sonar-based detection device, but we'd be borrowing it from one of his friends. An old house like this would make the perfect location for trying out that kind of tool. I hoped to get us into Oak Grove sooner rather than later. I couldn't shake the feeling that whatever was going on at Kali Oka Road had something to do with that house. To my surprise, Sara answered Peter's phone. I winced at the sleepy sound of her voice. I stared at the phone screen. Had I dialed the wrong number?

"Where's Pete, Sara?"

"Hold on," she said without offering any explanation of what just happened. I reminded myself that just last night I'd rejected her.

"Morning, champ," Pete said with a hint of something that sounded like sarcasm. But then that was his fallback position. He was the kind of guy who'd take the first swing, especially if he knew you had a good chance of beating him. Or if he was in the wrong. There was no doubt that a part of me would love to beat his ass, but we lived in the twenty-first century and I wasn't in kindergarten. I was the boss.

"Meeting with the folks from Oak Grove Plantation this morning. If I can get us in there I'd like to try the sonar. What do you think? Lots of old houses have hidden wall spaces, hidden rooms. I don't want to leave any stone unturned."

"I'll call Gavin and see if we can get it today. Do you think we'll get in there tonight?" His tone changed immediately. The only thing Peter Broadus loved more than tweaking my nose about Sara was a house investigation.

"That's what I'm hoping."

"I'll check with him and text you."

"All right, later."

I hung up and made the drive to Kali Oka Road. Like before, I was impressed with the wildness of the area. It was like the place refused to step into the present. Sure, there were houses scattered here and there and the inevitable light poles and street signs, but there was plenty of scraggly underbrush and acres of dense trees. And every so often there was a hidden path weaving crookedly into what used to be a historic forest. There weren't too many places downtown where you could experience this type of wildness. As one who believed in ghosts, I thought it seemed like the perfect place to find one.

"Hi. You must be Midas. I'm Junior Harlen, and this is my wife, Barbara."

"Yes, I am. Nice to meet you both. Thanks for meeting me and letting me take a look around."

"Oh, when I told Barbara you wanted to come check the place out, there was no denying her. She's into all that supernatural stuff. Me, not so much. I've never seen a ghost, but her sister sees them all the time. Doesn't she, Boo?"

"Stop, Junior. You're going to have this man thinking she's crazy. But then again, maybe you wouldn't. You might be just the guy my sister needs to talk to. We saw that television report about your group. Good work...I always knew that lighthouse was haunted."

I didn't argue with her. We'd not declared the lighthouse haunted, but it didn't seem like a good time to correct her. "I'd be happy to listen to her story. Did she have a supernatural experience?"

"I wish I could tell you all about it, but I have to ask her permission first. She's a very private person, and she'd kill me dead if I spoke out of turn. But you came to see Oak Grove today. Can you imagine what a lovely place this was when it was first built? We're looking forward to putting her back together."

"Come on. We'll take you on a tour," Junior said with a polite grin.

I followed the friendly couple through the gate and onto the property.

"Hard to believe this will be the talk of the town soon, but we plan on making it just that. In fact, Barbara would love to turn Oak Grove into a bed-and-breakfast. What do you think, Midas? Does this place have enough of a reputation to make it as a bed-and-breakfast? People seem to like this haunted stuff."

"Some people do. But I know plenty of people who run from anything labeled haunted."

"Even if the place isn't haunted, it feels that way. And the stories about Oak Grove are amazing," Barbara said, her brown eyes wide with excitement.

We stood in the front room, huddled together and talking in low whispers as if someone could hear us. "What kind of things have people experienced here? What stories have you heard?" I couldn't help but glance around. There was fresh paint on the walls and new carpet runners down a long hallway that sprawled in front of us. An elegant chandelier glowed warmly above us.

Junior raised his eyebrows at Barbara as she continued, "So many! The most popular story seems to be the one about the man who hangs around here. Apparently, he was a slave here and had a big old hulking frame. He's seen on the porch, in the windows and on the property surrounding the house."

"What about in the woods? Anyone see him there?"

"Sometimes, but never too far from the house. It's like he's watching over the place. He stays close. Now the ghost out in the woods is the Lady in White. She's never seen inside here, she's always where the forest used to be — what's left now is hardly the size of the original forest, but it's still quite wooded. She walks through there and down to the bridge. They say she cries the whole way. In fact, my cousin once saw her as he was driving across it. Said she was just standing in the center of the bridge, holding what looked like a bundle. He rolled down the window to ask her if she needed any help, but then she disappeared. Oh, and the other thing we hear about are the ghost lights. You know, round orbs of light? They see them all over Kali Oka Road. There's an old cemetery out back here, and they like to appear there. I saw one here once when we first started looking at the house. At first, I thought maybe it was light from a car, but it was the middle of the day! It bounced through the kitchen and out the window. My stars! Liked to have given me a heart attack."

"I can imagine. Let me ask you this, have you ever seen any unusual birds?"

Junior and Barbara looked puzzled. "You mean like a woodpecker?" he asked.

"More like an owl. A big dark one, maybe larger than normal."

"No, but I wouldn't doubt if we had a barn owl or two on the property. Lots of mice to snack on in these fields and such."

"My team and I would enjoy investigating Oak Grove. If we find anything, we'll be happy to put it in writing if that helps you at all. There's enough history here to believe that something could be here. I'm certainly not going to dismiss it if there is, but give us a chance to investigate."

"What do you do on these investigations?" Junior asked. "I hope you don't use Ouija boards. I'd have to object to that. I'm not afraid of a ghost or two, but I don't want to tinker with those creepy things."

It wasn't the first time I'd been asked that question. "No, sir. We don't use Ouija boards. We use scientific devices like this EMF detector." I pulled the small item from my pocket and showed it to the couple. I flipped on the device and waved it around. "See this? This meter tells me if there are shifts in the electromagnetic field. If there are spikes or surges, it usually means one of two things: there's an electrical appliance nearby or there's movement in the electromagnetic field. We believe ghosts pull on electricity and other power sources when they want to manifest."

"Oh no," Barbara said as she stared at the device. "I think you forgot to charge the battery."

"Not a problem. I have a fresh one here." I swapped out the battery and demonstrated how to use the machine again and then handed it to her. "Just wave it like this, but move it slowly."

Junior watched us with some amusement. His wife didn't pay him any attention. "Look, honey. I'm a ghost hunter! Shoot! This one is dead too."

"That can't be right. I charged it before I got here." I took the battery out and popped it back in. Nope. Dead as a doornail. "Strange." I glanced around the room suspiciously. It was starting to feel cold in here, much colder than it should have been. Barbara shivered beside me.

"All right, honey," Junior said. He turned to me. "We better get going if we're going to meet our son for lunch. Airport Boulevard is always busy this time of day. Let's get going." We headed out the door, and Junior locked it behind us. "What time do you want to meet us here?"

"About five o'clock? That will give us time to set up and investigate before it gets too late."

"All right. How late will you stay?"

"Usually we wrap up around two."

"In the morning?" Barbara asked, sounding shocked.

"Yes, ma'am. We find that twelve to two are the most supernaturally active times."

"Really? I heard that three was the witching hour," Junior added.

"Yes, sir. I believe that too. That's why I'm out of here by then."

"Seriously?" Barbara's voice shook.

"No, ma'am. I'm just kidding. To be honest, we're usually tired by then. Most of my team members have day jobs, and I try to respect their time. They are all volunteers."

Junior nodded. "I see. Well, we don't stay up that late. I'll leave you the key; just make sure you lock up when you're done. We have a lot of looky-loo's who like to come around. I can't blame them for being curious, what with all the rumors about ghosts, but I don't want them vandalizing the house. How long do you think it will be before you have the results of your investigation?"

"A few days. After we're done investigating, we'll review every camera and audio device thoroughly."

"That's good."

Junior took off his hat and scratched his head. "Tell me again why you want to explore Oak Grove. You mentioned Ranger Shaw, that's the boy who lost his girlfriend over by the bridge?"

"Yes, sir. Ranger's really sick…lung cancer has just about taken him out, but Melissa's still on his mind. He needs to know what happened to her. And I imagine he'd like to clear his name before he passes."

Junior slapped his cap back on. "I can see where a man would want to do that. It's all right with us if you search the house. I don't think the girl is here, but if it helps Ranger…"

"Thank you for allowing us to come. Like you, I'm not sure that the house is related at all to Ranger's experience, but I would like to get to the truth for him and for Melissa's family."

"Glad we could help him. Well, call us if you need us. And please be careful."

"Always. Thank you both."

It had been a long time since I'd been this excited about an investigation. We were actually going to check out Oak Grove. That was amazing. I turned the car onto Kali Oka Road and hit the Bluetooth on my dashboard to call Josh. "Get everything ready and pack extra batteries. I had a serious power drain on the EMF."

"Get out! Seriously?"

"Yeah. I'll meet you guys at GCP at three-thirty. Can you call everyone else?"

"Sure." I heard Sierra in the background. Josh said, "Ugh, Sierra. You're so nosey. She wants to know if she should call Cassidy in too."

"No. I'll call her myself."

"All right. Later." Josh hung up, and I headed to Cassidy's place.

I hoped I was doing the right thing.

Chapter Seventeen—Cassidy

I slept like a lumberjack for a while, but at five in the morning I was up and thinking about the painting. I hovered in front of the now-dry canvas with a brush in my hand but didn't know what to do next. One more drop of paint on this canvas felt wrong. It didn't need anything else. With sleepy eyes, I spotted one especially dark spot on the canvas. I wet the brush and rubbed the spot, hoping to lighten it up a bit.

No sooner had my brush touched the canvas than my surroundings changed; they melted away like crayons in a microwave. Now I wasn't in my chilly loft apartment. I was standing inside Oak Grove. How I knew that, I wasn't exactly sure.

Oh my God! Now what do I do?

I resisted the urge to call out because I didn't want anyone to know I was here. I wasn't supposed to be here. This was wrong. Completely wrong! As I was trying to determine what to do next, hide or run out of the house, a breeze swirled around me, like a mini tornado on a country road. I spun around just in time to see a dark figure rushing toward me. It was the man I'd seen on the porch of Oak Grove when Sara was with me. His face was taut and his hands stiff at his side. The next thing I knew he walked through me without seeing me. My stomach felt like a pulled rubber band, stretched and ready to pop. I gasped as I crumpled to my knees trying to regain my composure. I stood still for a few seconds until the sensation ceased. I watched as the man Aurelia called Cope walked quickly up the stairs.

I was looking at a ghost! No, that wasn't right. He wasn't the ghost—I was. I was in the past, not the present. I stared at my hands. They didn't seem unusual at all. Not ghostly, not invisible. But obviously Cope hadn't seen me.

Voices from a nearby room tore my attention away.

"You aren't going to throw me out of Oak Grove like a pile of garbage, Bernard. I got you here. I did everything you asked. It was me—and my power— that got you your fine wife and all your money."

"Like any pack mule, Hattie, you've served your purpose, and now it's time to put you out to pasture." I heard a clicking sound and then something crash to the ground, like smashed ceramic or porcelain. "What did you say to me? Are you calling me a mule?"

"Leave Oak Grove, or I'll have Cope throw you out on the road."

I shimmied closer to the open door. I could see a man in a brown suit leaning over a desk. He had neatly combed brown hair that came together in a wave at the left side of his head. He wore a blue and brown vest with brown dress pants and a pressed long-sleeved blue shirt. If I were to paint him, I would certainly include pink for his cheeks; it appeared as if he'd had a few belts before this meeting. This had to be Bernard Davis. I couldn't see the woman yet, but I could hear the swishing of her skirts as she moved around the room. They were voluminous and black, shiny — like that freaky owl.

"Go ahead and call your dog, Bernard. I've got something that will take care of him."

"Hattie, where did you get that? That's not a toy, my dear. Set the gun down now."

"You don't command me, Bernard Davis. I'm not some lily-white, pasty-faced coward that you can treat like a field hand. I won't be manhandled or abused in any kind of way." I heard the clicking of metal.

"Hattie, put the gun down. I understand how upsetting this is for you, but you have to see that it isn't possible to continue. You can't stay here. What we had is over, but we can remain friends, my dear. And I am of course fully prepared to compensate you. How much would you like? A hundred, two hundred?"

She didn't say anything, but I heard her high heels on the wooden floor of Bernard's office. He moved away from the desk but never turned his back on her. She moved into my view, and I studied her as any good artist would. Hattie's dark hair shone in the lamplight. It was so dark it was almost blue. I could see her profile. She was probably thirty-five with smooth skin and a full bottom lip. Her high-collared black gown revealed nothing, and she looked stiff and matronly except for the ruby red earrings that dangled from her ears.

"I want everything, Bernard. If you want me to go away, to leave and never come back, I want it all. You owe it to me. Think about what I've done for you. All the bodies I've put in the ground. All the spells I've cast. And you think you can send me away?"

"Hattie, put the gun down. Let's be reasonable. You want me to give you my entire fortune? That's not possible. You'd leave me penniless."

"That's better than leaving you and your progeny dead, isn't it? You honestly love that little monster, don't you?" Her steely voice dropped into a whisper. "He'll be a little monster, just like his father. If you do this to me, I promise you I'll kill him — and Aurelia." I moved closer to hear her better when the floorboard squeaked under my feet. "Who's there?" Hattie called in my direction. I caught my breath. She heard me!

At that moment, I heard the sound of bodies crashing to the floor. Hattie screamed as they struggled beneath the desk. It was only a matter of seconds before it was all over. The shot exploded in the house, and I could smell the gunpowder. Nobody moved. Perhaps they were both dead. I raced up the stairs to see Cope leading Aurelia and her wiggling, blanketed bundle down the hall to a back stair, obviously one used by servants or slaves.

"You have to go now! This is your only chance." He rushed her down the hall, looking over his shoulder nervously.

"Cope! What have you done with her, you bastard!" Hattie's shrill scream pierced the quiet of the house.

"Go for the bridge. I'll meet you there!" Cope shoved Aurelia away from him in the direction of the woods.

"No! She'll send that bird! What about the baby? What if she gets the baby?" Aurelia's thin face crumpled with fear.

"Run, Aurelia!" Cope shouted at her.

Then the sound of Hattie's anguished scream rang through the house. She wept loudly and called Bernard's name repeatedly. I hung on the porch for a few seconds, unsure what my next move was. Hattie had heard me once—what if she could see me too? My heart beat so fast, a reminder that I was indeed still very much alive.

Aurelia flew across the dusty yard. The moon rose high, and the sound of cicadas filled the night.

"I'll kill you!" Hattie shouted as she practically fell down the porch steps. "Get out of the way, Cope. I'll kill you dead."

He didn't waste any time, launching himself toward her and gripping her hands. His eyes widened with desperation, but Hattie was strong.

All I could think was, "Aurelia!" As they struggled I watched the frail-looking woman and her bundle disappear into the woods, and I ran behind her. Fear crept up my spine, and I prayed that she wasn't going to do what I thought she was.

Could Aurelia feel so desperate that she would harm her own baby? Was she so full of fear that she would do anything to protect him from Hattie?

Don't let it be true! It can't be true!

I passed through the yard and into the woods. Aurelia's dark hair flew behind her, and the baby began to whimper and cry. She was very near the road, and there was no sign of the bird. As she stepped off the sandy path and onto the moist peat, a gunshot reverberated through the air.

She froze on the path, clutching the crying baby. "Cope?" I thought for a second she would run back to Oak Grove. If she did, she would surely be killed. That is, if Hattie had survived. The danger remained. I could feel it in the air, and it was coming for Aurelia.

"Run!" I shouted to her instinctively. Her dark eyes grew large—she must have heard me! She broke and ran toward the road, and I ran with her. As she ran she mumbled a prayer.

I could see the bridge now. A thick fog had rolled in over the creek below. Panting now, Aurelia stopped to catch her breath. Then the tears came. "Cope!" she called back. The baby was screaming at the top of his lungs. From the woods not too far off, I heard the sound of wings rustling. It was the owl! It was flying toward her.

She disappeared into the fog, but I heard the baby continue to cry. Aurelia wasn't moving, judging by the sound of the screams. I prayed to God that I wouldn't hear a splash. "Run, Aurelia! She's coming!" I yelled into the night.

Someone broke branches just a few feet away from me. All I could do was flee. I ran into the fog, and everything began to fade. All of it. The crying of the baby. The sound of the cicadas. The breaking of the branches. I woke up breathing heavily with tears in my eyes.

Someone was knocking on my door. I flung it open, anxious to make human contact. With a living human and not the ghosts of the past.

It was Midas.

Without a word, I put my arms around his neck and cried.

Chapter Eighteen—Midas

My team waited in the conference area while I fumbled around my desk looking for my keys to Oak Grove. I'd just put them here. I couldn't be so scatterbrained that I'd leave them lying around for anyone to grab. But then again, who would steal them? I trusted everyone here.

Well, almost everyone. The sound of Pete's voice booming through the other room set my nerves on edge. Both Pete and Sara made me nervous, actually. I didn't trust them. Not anymore.

"Hi, you lose something?" Sara dangled a small clump of silver-toned keys near her head.

Speak of the devil.

"Yeah, I did. Where did you find them?"

"On the floor out there. You must be getting senile, Midas."

"That's not funny," I complained like a bear with a sore paw. She slapped a file folder on my desk and stood with her hands on her curved hips.

"Get over it, Romeo. Don't get all cranky because you didn't get any sleep last night. Do you even know who she is?" I assumed she was talking about Cassidy. I stalked to the door and closed it.

"She told you who she is. She's Cassidy Wright." I didn't bother to open the file folder. Sara was dying to tell me something, something I'd apparently missed. "She's filthy rich. Even richer than you, and that's saying something."

"What?" I said, staring at the pages.

"Seriously. You didn't know?"

"So what? She's got some money. Does it matter?"

"Does it matter? Well, it does to me. What else is she lying about?"

"Spell it out for me, Sara. No more damn head games! If you know something, spit it out. Otherwise, we have a meeting to attend."

Sara put an envelope on the table. My name was typed neatly on the outside. "This is for you. I'm taking that offer. I'll sell you my share for the figure you proposed. I want to be done with you."

"Fine. Is that it?" Her anger mystified me. She was the one who broke us up. Was I supposed to live in a monastery now?

"I guess so. It's as good as done." Her mouth drew up in a tight line.

"What do you want, Sara? You wanted to go, so go. Am I supposed to die because you decided to move on? What the hell do you want from me?"

"You know what I wanted. How I wanted this all to end. I guess you found a younger, richer model.

One who thinks the sun and the moon rise over your big, strong shoulders."

Walking back to the door completely frustrated, I said to her in a low voice, "You can be a real bitch sometimes, Sara." I half expected something to hit me in the back of the head, but it never happened. In fact, when we walked into the meeting room we were the sunshine couple again. Sara was all smiles when. She turned the hallway lights off and closed the door. As was our habit she locked the front door too and pulled the blinds closed. I don't know why we did it, but we always had.

I took my place at the head of the table. "We've got so much to cover, but I think we should start with…"

"Hold on, Midas," Sara interjected. "I have a bit of news I'd like to share with the team."

My stare didn't deter her, and she stood at the other end of the conference table now. I didn't give her permission, but I didn't try and stop her either. She was still co-owner of Gulf Coast Paranormal. At least for now. Hopefully she wouldn't drive a stake through the heart of our baby.

"As everyone knows, I'm going to work on a television project soon. It's an exciting time, but there's so much to do. Although I'm not scheduled to begin filming for a few months, I am making the move to California. I've found a great apartment and am anxious to get to know my new co-workers. Tonight will be my last investigation with you all. I've loved every minute of this; it's been such a rush. And to investigate in my hometown has been a dream come true. So thanks to you all."

"Congratulations, Sara! Oh my gosh! That's so terrific." Sierra hopped up, her long blond hair bouncing as she scrambled to hug her occasional friend, sometimes enemy. They held one another for a few seconds. I would never figure those two out. Josh and Cassidy stared at me, and Peter was visibly bored. Still, I wasn't going to interrupt this moment for Sara. If she wanted to go out like this, that was her business.

"Congratulations, Sara. That sounds exciting!" Cassidy was smiling and didn't seem to notice the icy tension in the room.

"And I'm going with her," Peter added in his typical bored-sounding voice.

"Are you going to be on the show too?" Cassidy asked after a near full minute of silence.

"Kind of. They want a technical guy, and I happened to have the credentials they were looking for. I think I'll put some of my ideas to work...with a bigger budget."

"I can't think of a better idea," I said in an equally wooden voice. Sierra hopped back in her chair and pouted.

"What the hell, Pete? You're leaving too?" Josh sounded particularly perturbed, but then again, any change in his routine bothered him. Unless he was the one to initiate the chaos; then he was all right with it.

"All right, let's stay focused on the task at hand. Midas, any word about Ranger? Did his son call?" Sierra's attempt to change the subject worked like a charm. As it always did. Even though she was the youngest in our group, she was often the most grown-up. Thank goodness, because I was ready to clobber Peter Broadus.

"His son picked up his truck, but so far Ranger hasn't come home. Ranger's most recent doctor's appointment didn't go so well. The treatment wasn't working like they hoped it would, and Steve isn't sure if his dad is really in trouble or just upset. He's filing a missing persons report in the morning, but maybe Ranger might have gone to see an old drinking buddy from high school."

"Why would he leave his truck?" Sierra asked curiously.

"That I don't know," I replied.

"That's just weird." Josh tapped his pen on the table. "Now the client is missing? Maybe we should let the police handle this, Midas."

"I promised Ranger we would investigate. He doesn't have much time, so I'm not willing to wait.

Hopefully we'll get some answers for him. And on that note, Cassidy had something happen last night. She had another encounter with the painting and saw some things that might help us."

"You're just full of magic, aren't you, Cassidy dear?" Sara's snide comment didn't sit well with me, but I chose to ignore her.

"After hearing about what happened to her, I think I know what our plan is for the house. For the rest of the property, I want to see what we can find out about the bird and Melissa's disappearance."

"What happened, Cassidy? I heard about the bird flying into your apartment. What else happened?" Josh was leaning forward, completely tuned in to the current conversation.

"Something is trying to communicate with me. I was there, last night, after Midas left. I fell asleep and traveled back to the night Bernard was killed. I can't help but feel like someone is leading me to reveal the truth about that place."

"Who?" Sara asked with another tinge of sarcasm. "Like a spirit guide?"

"Hey, that's not a joke," Josh said. "I happen to believe in spirit guides, and there's definitely a kind of energy that leads sensitives and mediums. How many times has Sierra had a hunch about something and it turned out to be right? We still believe in the supernatural here, don't we?"

Sara pursed her lips at him in a half-frown. "I'm just asking a question, Joshua. Aren't we still allowed to do that?"

So like Sara to make this about her. "Go ahead, Cassidy," I said. "Tell them what you saw this time, and don't leave anything out. Everyone, save your questions until the end."

For the next fifteen minutes, the team and I listened to Cassidy's retelling of her experience. I was getting tired of calling it that, but I didn't know what else to call it. I'd heard of people touching objects and getting sensations before but never an artist stepping back in time through her artwork.

At the end, everyone was mystified. Sara had her notebook out, and Sierra was tapping on the computer. They did their best to verify what they'd heard. "It's as good as anything we've learned, and it does fall within the realm of possibility. It would fit the narrative. Did the Harlens say the house was haunted?"

"They've heard stories of Cope being seen on the porch, but Barbara's sister has had some other experiences. I haven't had the chance to speak with her and get details."

"Oh, that reminds me." Cassidy dug in her purse and pulled out a digital voice recorder. I recognized it as one of ours. "There's something on here, Sara. From the other day. I cued it up."

With an astonished look, Sara took the recorder and hit play. We heard Cassidy ask questions, and then a voice turned up. It was a woman's voice I didn't recognize.

"Holy crap!" Sara said, rewinding it again and again. "Let's put it on your computer, Sierra. If we amplify it, maybe we can figure out what she's saying. It's definitely a female voice."

Sierra grabbed a cord and in a few seconds played the audio. We listened a few more times, and then it hit me. "I know what she's saying."

"What?" Cassidy asked as she held her breath in anticipation.

"Don't say anything, Midas," Sara said with her hand up. "Grab the headset. Everyone take a listen and write it down. Let's not influence one another here."

We did just that, but I was pretty confident in what I heard. After a few minutes, I picked up the slips of paper and read them aloud. Not everyone got what she said, just three of us, Sierra, Peter and me.

"Over the bridge."

We listened again, together this time. Everyone agreed that was what she said. It made my hair stand up, even after hearing it half a dozen times.

"I didn't know what she was saying until you said it, but I can tell you for sure that's Aurelia Davis,"

Cassidy said with confidence. "Is she saying she made it over the bridge? Is that what that means?"

"I hope so," Sierra said with a grimace, "not 'I went over the bridge.'"

"All right. Let's pack up. We know who the players might be, but let's stay open to the possibility that it could also be someone else. And if Cassidy's story is correct, at least two murders happened here. Be careful, everyone."

With that, we packed up and headed for Kali Oka Road. Time to face the ghosts of the past.

Chapter Nineteen—Cassidy

I helped Peter set up cameras and tried not to get in the way. It was nice out; at least we had that going for us. But the sun would go down soon, and we'd be in the dark with Hattie and Bernard Davis. If they showed up. Maybe they wouldn't. Maybe this had all been a dream.

Not a chance.

I unrolled the cable and followed Peter around, hoping to chit-chat with him about his upcoming move to Hollywood. It was obvious that his news had hit Midas and the rest of the team like a ton of bricks. I wasn't completely sure about the team dynamics, but it had the "kids in a messy divorce" vibe to it. It reminded me to keep a business head about myself and cry less on Midas' shoulders. Normally I wasn't the kind of girl to rush things, but these past few days had taken me by surprise. And it had all started because the power went out on my block and I was too impatient to wait for it to come back on. What would have happened if I hadn't met the GCP team?

"Over here, dreamer." Peter's snappy attitude didn't bother me too much. He was nothing compared to Uncle Derek. Which reminded me, I hadn't called him yet. I wondered why the heck he'd send Mike to my house. If he'd sent him at all. Perhaps Mike was lying about that. He'd taken to lying quite a bit during the last part of our relationship. Maybe he'd been lying the whole time. Who the heck knows?

"Sorry. I guess I zoned out."

"You getting some vibes or something?" Peter smiled up at me. He was on the ground wrapping cords together.

"No. I never get vibes. Do you? Is that your secret power?"

"Nope. My secret power, Cassidy, is pissing people off." Sara walked past him waving a gadget, completely oblivious to our conversation. Or she was ignoring me. Either way was fine with me. I was glad she was leaving, actually. Wasn't sure she'd ever warm up to me. As they say, "Two redheads in a room is one too many." Peter openly stared at her behind as she strolled down the hall. He seemed lost in his own dirty thoughts for a moment and then smiled at me again.

"Poor kid. You've lost your heart to the wonderful world of the supernatural, haven't you? It happens to us all. At least in the beginning."

It was my turn to get an attitude now. I followed him through the kitchen door. "What do you mean by that? I haven't lost my heart."

"Don't get all defensive. I'd think you'd have thicker skin after all you've been through. I just meant these investigations are exciting at first, but over time it wears on you. You'll see. If you stick with it."

"I don't think it's like that. I'm not experiencing puppy love, Peter. I'm just trying to get a handle on what's happening to me. And if I can help someone on top of that, then that's even better."

"Hey, you don't have to explain anything to me. Would you mind going back upstairs and grabbing that black case I left up there? It's the one with the skull sticker on the side. I left my battery pack for this thing in there. I'd appreciate it."

"Sure," I said, glad to get away from him. How had I gotten stuck with him anyway? I jogged back up the stairs, focusing on the task at hand. I looked where we left it, but it wasn't there anymore. Someone must have moved it. But where? "Anyone up here?" I called down the clean hallway. Someone had taken a great deal of care to refinish the place. The wooden floors were lovely, and there was a deep burgundy runner down the center of the hallway. Above us were two chandeliers, evenly spaced to provide maximum lighting down the long hallway. There weren't too many paintings on the walls, but I'd heard the Harlens hadn't had the place too long. So far, though, what they'd accomplished was pretty nice.

I heard a shuffling of papers, like someone was writing at a desk or moving a large amount of mail around. Kind of like I do when I become inundated with junk mail. I am notorious for not opening mail when I should. I solved that problem last year and hired an accountant. He paid bills for me and made sure my lights stayed on.

"Hello?" I called again, but there was no answer. I poised in the hallway hoping to hear the sound again. Just when I thought I'd imagined it—there it was again. I walked down the hallway and stopped outside the last door on the right. There was the case! I walked in the room, surprised to find it here. This room was unfinished, with a bed frame, an old dresser and some paint cans in it. I reached for the case.

How did it get in here?

Out of the corner of my eye, I saw movement, a piece of a garment, white and flowing. I stood up immediately and forgot about Peter's case. I looked around the room and saw nothing significant, but I could clearly see out the untreated windows. I ran to the window and saw Aurelia fleeing from the yard, just like in my dreams. Unlike my dreams, Cope wasn't in the scene, or at least I couldn't see him. But she was running, her face full of hair, her loose hair swirling around her like dark ropes.

It was like watching a movie in slow motion. I suddenly wanted to run after her, protect her, make sure she was okay.

The next thing I knew I was barreling downstairs past Peter, who must have gotten tired of waiting on me. "Hey! Did you find it? What's wrong?" I didn't answer. All my focus was on Aurelia.

Peter called me rude but didn't try to stop me. I was glad. I ran out the back of the house, away from the Gulf Coast Paranormal vans and toward Kali Oka Road — and Aurelia. It was dark out, even though the sun had been in the sky just a few minutes ago. I couldn't think about that right now. I kept running. I could see her now. She was ahead of me and turning back occasionally to see if Cope followed her.

"Keep running, Aurelia!" I shouted like a madwoman. Unlike that day, the day when she left Oak Grove, the moon was up, shining its bright light on the woods and the surrounding area. The Kali Oka forest was full of magnolias, bays, pine trees and live oaks. There were many hills and creeks, and if you weren't careful in the dark, you might land in the water. But Aurelia didn't change her track. She was running the same way she had before. It was as if she were caught in some kind of time loop. Maybe that's what ghosts were? Souls locked in an infinite loop until they accomplished their deed. I saw her face as she screamed in anguish, "Cope! Come with me! You said together!" The gunshot sounded in my ears, but it all still played out in slow motion.

I fell on the path but didn't break my gaze. I felt as if I looked away she would disappear. I couldn't let that happen. I wanted to see this all the way through, in real time.

The bridge was in view now. It was smaller and made completely of heavy wooden beams. Obviously this was the old bridge. Beneath it, I heard the water running over the rocks. Again cicadas' songs filled the trees, and bullfrogs joined in. The fog I'd seen before appeared now, and for a moment Aurelia was lost in it. I screamed her name, and the sound was in slow motion too! I glanced behind me and saw Hattie, with the evil bird perched on her arm ready to do her bidding. She was screaming profanities and promising to do evil to Aurelia and her baby. Aurelia didn't wait for her to arrive. She stood on the bridge hidden in the fog.

"Run, Aurelia! Please! Run now! You can make it!"

She didn't seem to hear me. I saw her look over the side of the bridge. The baby began to wail again. Surely she wouldn't do that! She would not sacrifice her child to save herself, nor would she kill the baby out of some sort of strange idea that he would be better off dead.

Then I heard what I wanted to hear. Her tearful voice screaming, "Cope! Over the bridge! Come over the bridge!" And then she was gone, disappearing completely in the fog. The baby was crying in the distance now, but soon the cries faded completely. Then Hattie appeared and right behind her a bloodied Cope. They struggled, but Hattie was no match for Cope's strength. Before he pushed her off the bridge, she laughed in his face. "I've already sent my night eagle. He'll take care of the baby and the woman too. She's as good as dead now!" And with a final push from Cope, she went screaming into the water below.

With tears and great heartbreak, he cried out, "Aurelia! Where are you? Oh please, oh please, God! Have mercy!" He ran back across the bridge and searched the water below for Aurelia and the baby. Suddenly he disappeared, and Hattie's body was gone too.

"Cassidy!" Midas shouted. "What are you doing here? I've been looking all over for you. You can't run off without telling someone where you're going." He hugged me to his chest. "Are you all right?" he asked somewhat more softly than before.

"Yes, I'm okay. Aurelia's gone. She made it to the other side. She left here. Thank you, God! She left here! But Cope doesn't know. He never found her. He doesn't know she's okay."

"Then let's go tell him."

"Let's go, Midas."

Chapter Twenty—Cassidy

"There you are!" Sierra shouted when we returned to the house. "Crazy girl. Don't do that again, please! We can't afford to lose another team member." She put her arm around me protectively.

"I know what Aurelia's words on the recording mean. She wants Cope to know she made it. She wants him to come over the bridge." I was beyond caring if they believed me or not. "If there's some way we can play that recording for him, maybe he'll be free from here and she can stop haunting these woods."

Midas agreed with me. "All right, let's divide into two teams. Sierra, Cassidy and I will stay in the house, and the rest of you will go out in the backyard. We all have a copy of that EVP. Let's see if we can summon Cope back and let him hear the truth for himself. Play it!"

Sierra had gotten quiet and glanced around. I didn't know her well, but I could tell she was sensing something. Something we could not see. "That's not going to work. It has to be Cassidy. He's allowed her to see him three times now. That's for a reason. He trusts her, I think. So does Aurelia. Just talk to him, Cassidy, see if he'll come back."

"All right," I said as I cleared my throat. Everyone else found a spot to sit, and I remained standing. "Cope! My name is Cassidy, and these are my friends. We're your friends. Aurelia is my friend too. She gave me a message to give to you. Cope?"

I didn't hear anything, but the tension grew. "Sierra? You feeling anything, sweetie?" Joshua asked, squeezing her hand.

"He's close," she answered in a whisper.

I sat in the only vacant seat. It had gotten dark in here, and quickly. I couldn't see my hand in front of my face. "Please trust us, Cope. I know it's hard, but we're your friends. I promise we don't want to hurt you."

Sierra waved her audio recorder. It beeped to show we'd caught something. We played it back, and it had one word on it. It was unclear what that was, but it could have been "Aurelia..." in a whisper. I went with it.

"Yes, Aurelia. Our friend, your friend. She made it across the bridge, Cope. You saved her and the baby. You did it!"

Suddenly a ghostly light appeared in the hallway about three feet off the ground. It was like a white flame, burning away. Then it expanded suddenly, and a man was standing there, or the outline of a man. It was Cope! I gasped to see him looking so frightened and so alive. Even though it was just his outline, I could see the dark skin on his face and his expressive chocolate brown eyes. Joshua swore under his breath, and Midas stood so stiffly that he must have been an inch taller.

"I am Aurelia's friend. She told me to give you a message. May I give you that message, Cope?"

He didn't speak or nod, but the light at the center of him bounced once and he hovered and waited.

With nervous fingers, Sierra played the audio clip, turning it up as loud as possible. Aurelia's voice filled the room.

"Over the bridge!"

He opened his mouth to laugh, but I couldn't hear him. It was like he was stuck inside a soundproof box. He said something to me, but I couldn't make it out. Then he vanished, leaving behind a trace of smoke or an unearthly fog.

I cried, Sierra cried with me and Midas hugged us both. Joshua continued to mutter curse words while Sara and Peter sat in stunned silence. It was a good way to end my first investigation.

Epilogue—Cassidy

Sliding my feet into fluffy pink slippers I sauntered over to Kylie's painting and touched it with my fingers. *If only you'd speak to me, baby girl.* She didn't. I flipped on a nearby lamp to get a better view of the painting that I'd already seen at least ten thousand times now.

While I pondered the photo, I thought about the case. On the news last night Ranger Shaw was reported dead, killed by the same man who killed Melissa Hendricks, Beau Whisenhunt. Some kind of love triangle, only Ranger never knew that Melissa was stepping out on him. It had come to its full conclusion now. His son was a wreck, but at least he had answers. His father had been no murderer.

A memorial stone for Cope would go up soon, and Aurelia? Who knew where she ended up, but at least she had lived and made it across the bridge and never had to deal with Bernard again.

We didn't learn much else about the bird. Was the black owl really an evil animal or just a bird of prey that found a great opportunity to grab an unusual snack the night Melissa was killed on Kali Oka Road? But then again, if it wasn't a spirit animal, how could it scratch me all to pieces?

These were questions I'd have to think about a while. The Harlens were glad we'd cleared the house, but they asked us to keep it quiet. The people who came to their bed-and-breakfast later this summer would expect a ghost or two. They were happy we'd done what we did, though.

And now it's just you and me again, kiddo. I miss you, Kylie.

I'd memorized every square inch of the painting, but for the first time since the day I'd finished it, I felt like something was missing.

Yes, there was something missing! I hurried to blend the paints I would need and began tapping on the shape. Yes, just there! In the right-hand corner.

With a blend of blues, grays and bright white, I smoothed on the long spindly legs of a water tower. It had a wide umbrella tub and a few other small details like a rusting ladder and handrails. How had I missed that?

An hour later I was somewhat satisfied, except there was no name on the water tower. If only I could grab that name, snatch it out of my subconscious or wherever these things came from. I stood waiting, hoping. Nothing came. Eventually, I put the brush down and sat on the stool staring at the painting.

Yes, this was right. I had another clue. After all this time. Why? Why was I getting fresh information now?

Could it be because of my new association with Gulf Coast Paranormal? Was Kylie leading me to find her? If I ever stood a chance of doing that, it would be now with Sierra, Midas and the rest of the team. I didn't want my sister to be gone; I wanted her to be alive. With all my heart, I wanted that and believed it. But if she wasn't, if something had happened, I wanted to at least bring her home.

The phone rang and jostled me out of my reverie. I glanced at the clock. It was early but not too early. Almost eight o'clock.

"Hello?"

"Hi, Cassidy."

"Good morning, Midas."

"Hope I didn't wake you."

"No. I was up. I've been painting."

"Oh, anything I should know about?" he asked hopefully.

"Not yet, but I'll keep you posted. What's up?"

"How about meeting us at Demeter's? If you're up for it. We've got another case, and I think we could use your help."

I couldn't help but smile. It was nice to be needed somewhere. I hadn't quite made up my mind whether I would stay with Gulf Coast Paranormal. At least not until now. Now I knew the answer as plainly as I knew my name.

"Sure. I'm game. What time?"

"Nine o'clock. Don't be late."

"Won't be." I paused as I chewed my bottom lip thoughtfully. "And Midas?"

"Yes?"

"Thanks for the invite."

Without waiting for his answer to my hokey comment, I hung up the phone. With one last look at Kylie's pretty face, I swirled the brush in the water and set it in a jar to dry.

"Someday, little sister, I'm going to bring you home."

I reached out to touch the paint but drew my hand back. Midas had asked me not to be late. I'd tackle this later tonight. I could see where I'd missed a few things. There was a small building that needed to go there, just below the tower.

As I walked away to take my shower I whispered, "See you tonight, Kylie."

For the first time in a long time, I believed that I would.

More from M. L. Bullock

From the *Ultimate Seven Sisters Collection*

A smile crept across my face when I turned back to look at the pale faces watching me from behind the lace curtains of the girls' dormitory. I didn't feel sorry for any of them — all of those girls hated me. They thought they were my betters because they were orphans and I was merely the accidental result of my wealthy mother's indiscretion. I couldn't understand why they felt that way. As I told Marie Bettencourt, at least my parents were alive and wealthy. Hers were dead and in the cold, cold ground. "Worm food now, I suppose." Her big dark eyes had swollen with tears, her ugly, fat face contorting as she cried. Mrs. Bedford scolded me for my remarks, but even that did not worry me.

I had a tool much more effective than Mrs. Bedford's threats of letters to the attorney who distributed my allowance or a day without a meal. Mr. Bedford would defend me — for a price. I would have to kiss his thin, dry lips and pretend that he did not peek at my décolletage a little too long. Once he even squeezed my bosom ever so quickly with his rough hands but then pretended it had been an accident. Mr. Bedford never had the courage to lift up my skirt or ask me for a "discreet favor," as my previous chaperone had called it, but I enjoyed making him stare. It had been great fun for a month or two until I saw how easily he could be manipulated.

And now my rescuer had come at last, a man, Louis Beaumont, who claimed to be my mother's brother. I had never met Olivia, my mother. Not that I could remember, anyway, and I assumed I never would.

Louis Beaumont towered above most men, as tall as an otherworldly prince. He had beautiful blond hair that I wanted to plunge my hands into. It looked like the down of a baby duckling. He had fair skin — so light it almost glowed — with pleasant features, even brows, thick lashes, a manly mouth. It was a shame he was so near a kin because I would have had no objections to whispering "Embrasse-moi" in his ear. Although I very much doubted Uncle Louis would have indulged my fantasy. How I loved to kiss, and to kiss one so beautiful! That would be heavenly. I had never kissed a handsome man before — I kissed the ice boy once and a farmhand, but neither of them had been handsome or good at kissing.

For three days we traveled in the coach, my uncle explaining what he wanted and how I would benefit if I followed his instructions. According to my uncle, Cousin Calpurnia needed me, or rather, needed a companion for the season. The heiress would come out this year, and a certain level of decorum was expected, including traveling with a suitable companion. "Who would be more suitable than her own cousin?" he asked me with the curl of a smile on his regal face. "Now, dearest Isla," he said, "I am counting on you to be a respectable girl. Leave all that happened before behind in Birmingham — no talking of the Bedfords or anyone else from that life. All will be well now." He patted my hand gently. "We must find Calpurnia a suitable husband, one that will give her the life she's accustomed to and deserves."

Yes, indeed. Now that this Calpurnia needed a proper companion, I had been summoned. I'd never even heard of Miss Calpurnia Cottonwood until now. Where had Uncle Louis been when I ran sobbing in a crumpled dress after falling prey to the lecherous hands of General Harper, my first guardian? Where had he been when I endured the shame and pain of my stolen maidenhead? Where? Was I not Beaumont stock and worthy of rescue? Apparently not. I decided then and there to hate my cousin, no matter how rich she was. Still, I smiled, spreading the skirt of my purple dress neatly around me on the seat. "Yes, Uncle Louis."

"And who knows, ma petite Cherie, perhaps we can find you a good match too. Perhaps a military man or a wealthy merchant. Would you like that?" I gave him another smile and nod before I pretended to be distracted by something out the window. My fate would be in my own hands, that much I knew. Never would I marry. I would make my own future. Calpurnia must be a pitiful, ridiculous kind of girl if she needed my help to land a "suitable" husband with all her affluence.

About the *Ultimate Seven Sisters Collection*

When historian Carrie Jo Jardine accepted her dream job as chief historian at Seven Sisters in Mobile, Alabama, she had no idea what she would encounter. The moldering old plantation housed more than a few boxes of antebellum artifacts and forgotten oil paintings. Secrets lived there—and they demanded to be set free.

This contains the entire supernatural suspense series.

More from M. L. Bullock

From *The Tale of Nefret*

Clapping my hands three times, I smiled, amused at the half-dozen pairs of dark eyes that watched me entranced with every word and movement I made. "And then she crept up to the rock door and clapped her hands again…" *Clap, clap, clap.* The children squealed with delight as I weaved my story. This was one of their favorites, The Story of Mahara, about an adventurous queen who constantly fought magical creatures to win back her clan's stolen treasures.

"Mahara crouched down as low as she could." I demonstrated, squatting as low as I could in the tent. "She knew that the serpent could only see her if she stood up tall, for he had very poor eyesight. If she was going to steal back the jewel, she would have to crawl her way into the den, just as the serpent opened the door. She was terrified, but the words of her mother rang in her ears: 'Please, Mahara! Bring back our treasures and restore our honor!'"

I crawled around, pretending to be Mahara. The children giggled. "Now Mahara had to be very quiet. The bones of a hundred warriors lay in the serpent's cave. One wrong move and that old snake would see her and…catch her!" I grabbed at a nearby child, who screamed in surprise. Before I could finish my tale, Pah entered our tent, a look of disgust on her face.

"What is this? Must our tent now become a playground? Out! All of you, out! Today is a special day, and we have to get ready."

The children complained loudly, "We want to hear Nefret's story! Can't we stay a little longer?"

Pah shook her head, and her long, straight hair shimmered. "Out! Now!" she scolded the spokesman for the group.

"Run along. There will be time for stories later," I promised them.

As the heavy curtain fell behind them, I gave Pah an unhappy look. She simply shook her head. "You shouldn't make promises that you may not be able to keep, Nefret. You do not know what the future holds."

"Why must you treat them so? They are only children!" I set about dressing for the day. Today we were to dress simply with an aba—a sleeveless coat and trousers. I chose green as my color, and Pah wore blue. I cinched the aba at the waist with a thick leather belt. I wore my hair in a long braid. My fingers trembled as I cinched it with a small bit of cloth.

"Well, if nothing else, you'll be queen of the children, Nefret."

About *The Tale of Nefret*

Twin daughters of an ancient Bedouin king struggle under the weight of an ominous prophecy that threatens to divide them forever. Royal sibling rivalry explodes as the young women realize that they must fight for their future and for the love of Alexio, the man they both love. *The Tale of Nefret* chronicles their lives as they travel in two different directions. One sister becomes the leader of the Meshwesh while the other travels to Egypt as an unwilling gift to Pharaoh.

More from M. L. Bullock

From *Wife of the Left Hand*

Okay, so it was official. I *had* lost my mind. I turned off the television and got up from the settee. I couldn't explain any of it, and who would believe me? Too many weird things had happened today — ever since I arrived at Sugar Hill.

Just walk away, Avery. Walk away. That had always been good advice, Vertie's advice, actually.

And I did.

I took a long hot bath, slid into some comfortable pinstriped pajamas, pulled my hair into a messy bun and climbed into my king-sized bed.

All was well. Until about midnight.

A shocking noise had me sitting up straight in the bed. It was the loudest, deepest clock I had ever heard, and it took forever for the bells to ring twelve times. After the last ring, I flopped back on my bed and pulled the covers over my head. Would I be able to go back to sleep now?

To my surprise, the clock struck once more. What kind of clock struck thirteen? Immediately my room got cold, the kind of cold that would ice you down to your bones. Wrapping the down comforter around me, I turned on the lamp beside me and huddled in the bed, waiting…for something…

I sat waiting, wishing I were brave enough and warm enough to go relight a fire in my fireplace. It was so cold I could see my breath now. Thank God I hadn't slept nude tonight. Jonah had hated when I wore pajamas to bed. *Screw him!* I willed myself to stop thinking about him. That was all in the past now. He'd made his choice, and I had made mine.

Then I heard the sound for the first time. It was soft at first, like a kitten crying pitifully. Was there a lost cat here? That would be totally possible in this big old house. As the mewing sound drew closer, I could hear much more clearly it was not a kitten but a child. A little girl crying as if her heart were broken. Sliding my feet in my fuzzy white slippers and wrapping the blanket around me tightly, I awkwardly tiptoed to the door to listen. Must be one of the housekeepers' children. Probably cold and lost. I imagined if you wanted to, you could get lost here and never be found. Now her crying mixed with whispers as if she were saying something; she was pleading as if her life depended on it. My heart broke at the sound, but I couldn't bring myself to open the door and actually take a look. Not yet. I scrambled for my iPhone and jogged back to the door to record the sounds. How else would anyone believe me? Too many unbelievable things had happened today. With my phone in one hand, the edge of my blanket in my teeth to keep it in place and my free hand on the doorknob, I readied myself to open the door. I had to see who—or what—was crying in the hallway. I tried to turn the icy cold silver-toned knob, but it wouldn't budge. It was as if someone had locked me in. Who would do such a thing? Surely not Dinah or Edith or one of the other staff?

About *Wife of the Left Hand*

Avery Dufresne had the perfect life: a rock star boyfriend, a high-profile career in the anchor chair on a national news program. Until a serious threat brings her perfect world to a shattering stop. When Avery emerges from the darkness she finds she has a new ability — a supernatural one. Avery returns to Belle Fontaine, Alabama, to claim an inheritance: an old plantation called Sugar Hill. Little does she know that the danger has just begun.

More from M. L. Bullock

From *The Mermaid's Gift*

Dauphin Island had more than its share of weirdness—a fact illustrated by tomorrow's Mullet Toss—but it was home to me. It wasn't as popular as nearby Sand Island or Frenchman Bay, and we islanders clung to our small-town identity like it was a badge of honor. Almost unanimously, islanders refused to succumb to the pressure of beach developers and big-city politicians who occasionally visited our pristine stretches of sand with dollar signs in their eyes. No matter how they sweet-talked the town elders, they left unsatisfied time and time again, with the exception of a lone tower of condominiums that stood awkwardly in the center of the island. As someone said recently at our monthly town meeting, "We don't need all that hoopla." That seemed to be the general sense of things, and although I valued what they were trying to preserve, I didn't always agree with my fellow business owners and residents. Still, I was just Nike Augustine, the girl with a weird name and a love for french fries but most notably the granddaughter of the late Jack Augustine, respected one-time mayor of Dauphin Island. What did I know? I was too young to appreciate the importance of protecting our sheltered island. Or so I had been told. So island folk such as myself made the bulk of our money during spring break and the Deep Sea Fishing Rodeo in July. It was enough to make a girl nuts.

But despite this prime example of narrow-mindedness, I fit in here. Along with all the oddities like the island clock that never worked properly, the abandoned lighthouse that everyone believed was haunted and the fake purple shark that hung outside my grandfather's souvenir shop. I reminded myself of that when the overwhelming desire to wander overtook me, as it threatened to do today and had done most days recently. I had even begun to dream of diving into the ocean and swimming as far down as I could. Pretty crazy since I feared the water, or more specifically what swam hidden in the darkness. Another Nike eccentricity. Only my grandfather understood my reluctance, but he was no longer here to tell me I wasn't crazy. My fear of water separated me from my friends, who practically lived in or on the waters of the Gulf of Mexico or the Mobile Bay most of the year.

Meandering down the aisles of the souvenir shop, I stopped occasionally to turn a glass dolphin and rearrange a few baskets of dusty shells. I halfheartedly slapped the shelves with my dust rag and glanced at the clock again and again until finally the shark-tooth-tipped hands hit five o'clock. With a bored sigh, I walked to the door, turned the sign to Closed and flicked off the neon sign that glowed: "Shipwreck Souvenirs." I'd keep longer hours when spring break began, but for now it was 9 to 5.

I walked to the storeroom to retrieve the straw broom. I had to pay homage to tradition and make a quick pass over the chipped floor. I'd had barely any traffic today, just a few landlubbers hoping to avoid the spring breakers; as many early birds had discovered, the cold Gulf waters weren't warm enough to frolic in yet. Probably fewer than a dozen people had darkened my door today, and only half of those had the courtesy to buy something. With another sigh, I remembered the annoying child who had rubbed his sticky hands all over the inflatables before announcing to the world that he had to pee. I thanked my Lucky Stars that I didn't have kids. But then again, I would need a boyfriend or husband for that, right?

Oh, yeah. I get to clean the toilets, too.

I wondered what the little miscreant had left behind for me in the tiny bathroom. No sense in griping about it. It was me or no one. I wouldn't be hiring any help anytime soon. I grabbed the broom and turned to take care of the task at hand when I heard a suspicious sound that made me pause.

Someone was near the back door, rattling through the garbage cans. I could hear the metal lid banging on the ground. Might be a cat or dog, but it might also be Dauphin Island's latest homeless resident. We had a few, but this lost soul tugged at my heart-strings. I had never seen a woman without a place to live. So far she had refused to tell me her name or speak to me at all. Perhaps she was hard of hearing too? Whatever the case, it sounded as if she weren't above digging through my trash cans. Which meant even more work for me. "Hey," I called through the door, hoping to stop her before she destroyed it.

I had remembered her today as I was eating my lunch. I saved her half of my club sandwich. I had hoped I could tempt her to talk to me, but as if she knew what I had planned, she'd made herself scarce. Until now.

I slung the door open, and the blinds crashed into the mauve-painted wall. Nobody was there, but a torn bag of trash lay on the ground. I yelled in the direction of the cans, "Hey! You don't have to tear up the garbage! I have food for you. Are you hungry?"

I might as well have been talking to the dolphins that splashed offshore. Nobody answered me. "I know you're there! I just heard you in my trash. Come out, lady. I won't hurt you." Still nobody answered. I heard a sound like a low growl coming from the side of my store.

What the heck was that?

Immediately I felt my adrenaline surge. Danger stalked close. I ran to the back wall of my shop and flattened myself against the rough wood. I heard the growl again. Was that a possum? Gator? Rabies-crazed homeless lady? I knew I shouldn't have started binge-watching *The Walking Dead* this week. There was absolutely nothing wrong with my imagination. My mind reeled with the possibilities. After a few seconds I quietly reasoned with myself. I didn't have time for this. Time to face the beast — whatever it might be.

About *The Mermaid's Gift*

Nike Augustine isn't your average girl next door. She's a spunky siren but, thanks to a memory loss, doesn't know it — yet. By day, she runs a souvenir shop on Dauphin Island off the coast of Alabama, but a chance encounter opens her eyes to the supernatural creatures that call the island home, including a mermaid, a fallen goddess and a host of other beings. When an old enemy appears and attempts to breach the Sirens Gate, Nike and her friends must take to the water to prevent the resurrection of a long-dead relative…but the cost might be too high.

To make matters worse, Nike has to choose between longtime crush, Officer Cruise Castille and Ramara, a handsome supernaturate who has proven he's willing to lose everything — including his powers — for the woman he loves.

Read more from M.L. Bullock

The Seven Sisters Series

Seven Sisters
Moonlight Falls on Seven Sisters
Shadows Stir at Seven Sisters
The Stars that Fell
The Stars We Walked Upon
The Sun Rises Over Seven Sisters

The Idlewood Series

The Ghosts of Idlewood
Dreams of Idlewood
The Whispering Saint
The Haunted Child (forthcoming)

Return to Seven Sisters
(A Forthcoming Sequel Series to Seven Sisters)

The Roses of Mobile
A Garden of Thorns
All the Summer Roses
Blooms Torn Asunder
A Final Wreath of Roses

Cotton City Antiques
(A Forthcoming Seven Sisters Spinoff Series)

A Voice from Her Past
The Haunted Letter
Henri's Ghost Light
Missing Time in Mobile
Phantom Photos of Tomorrow
The Weeping of Angels

The Sirens Gate Series

The Mermaid's Gift
The Blood Feud
The Wrath of Minerva
The Lorelei Curse (forthcoming)
The Island Jinx (forthcoming)
The Fortunate Star (forthcoming)

The Southern Gothic Series

Being with Beau

To receive updates on her latest releases,
visit her website at MLBullock.com
and subscribe to her mailing list.

Made in the USA
Middletown, DE
30 October 2022